EarthShift

Judith Horky

Crystal Mountain Press
Pagosa Springs, Colorado

EarthShift
by Judy Horky

Published 2002

Published by
Crystal Mountain Press
5392 No. Pagosa Blvd.,
Pagosa Springs, CO 81147
http://www.earthshift.net

ISBN: 0-9711862-0-0

Cover photo: Jeff Bowen
Cover design: Tom Drews
Author photo: Jim Horky

Printed in the United States of America

ACKNOWLEDGMENTS

So many beings, both visible and invisible, assisted in the birth of ***EarthShift***.

I am extremely grateful for the friends and family members, too numerous to mention individually, who supported me throughout the creative process.

Heartfelt thanks go to my son, Tom, whose unrelenting encouragement and belief in me helped me believe in myself.

Blessings and gratitude to Karen Cook and Benu, Angela Mattey, and Tony Stubbs for their guidance and support.

I send love and appreciation to Mom and Dad in the spirit world—Mom for her love of books and the English language, and Dad for his encouragement and open mind.

My deepest gratitude goes to my husband and best friend, Jim, who has believed in me from the moment we met. His unwavering support, unconditional love and infinite patience are, indeed, priceless. He is my love, my soulmate, and as we experience the wind song of awakening together, our connection will always be, forever more, One with each other and All That Is.

Characters

The Family:

Julie and Dave Armstrong

Jon Cramer (Julie's son)

Steve and Megan Cramer (Julie's son and his wife)

Jesse and Michael Cramer (their 6-year-old twins)

Bill and Kathy Cramer (Julie's son)

Joey Cramer (their 5-year-old son)

Erica Cramer (their 1-year-old daughter)

Chris and Ellen Armstrong (Dave's son and daughter-in-law)

Jerry and Jean Mathews (Dave's daughter and son-in-law)

Angela Mathews (their infant daughter)

In the Spirit World:

Danny Cramer (Julie's infant son)

Kent and Irene Lockhart (Julie's father and mother)

Clarence Lockhart (Julie's uncle)

Rose (Nana) Armstrong (Dave's mother)

Friends and Guides:

Gabriel (Energy of the Archangel)

Dorado (Jesse's spiritual ET guide)

Ekor (Jon's dolphin friend)

Roger (Jon's young friend in hospital)

Rachel, Anna, Doug (friends of Julie and Dave)

Ray (Julie's ex-husband)

The Animals:

Max and Sandy (Julie and Dave's dogs)

Misty (Julie's bay)

Orion (Dave's gelding)

Rusty (Mike and Jesse's dog)

Foreword

The "Photon Belt" is a phenomenon composed of energy.
It is slowly sweeping through the galaxy
changing the electromagnetic field of Mother Earth
and life as we know it.

This Shift of the Ages has many names: The Awakening,
Ascension, the Tribulation, Transformation,
Armageddon, The Rapture, Transcendence
and The Book of Revelation, to name a few.
A rose by any other name is still a rose. The Shift *is* coming.

"Takoma" is an ancient word meaning a special place of power. It is a crossroad for the pathways of angels, guides, and teachers whose energies create a vortex of peace, love, and wisdom.

Welcome to the town of Takoma Springs, Wind Dancer Ranch, and Julie Armstrong and her family. As the winds touch down and Crystal Mountain shares its beauty and mysticism with all who "see," the emerging power of the Photon Energy forces the human race to face and deal with their fears and to accept the consequences of their choices.

The ***EarthShift*** has begun.

It shall be given to you according to your beliefs.

Prologue

Bill squirmed in his chair, sticky sweat dripping down his back as he adjusted his lanky six-foot-four frame in the small hard chair next to the video production console. The countdown had begun. TV cameras were focused and the satellite feed from the Oval Office in Washington was tracking. The President began speaking.

Bill's engineer, Tex, and his team were tense but capable of handling any emergency. Well, most any, Bill thought. He hadn't realized how much extra time would be eaten up by all the security measures for both equipment and crew, and his stomach was in knots. Live TV always raised his blood pressure. No re-takes, no editing. The damn power hits didn't help any, either.

He wondered what this "big announcement" was all about. Obviously it was important. Anything that pre-empted the almighty sitcoms had to be. Even more important at the moment was how things would go when Washington threw it to them in L.A. Bill's venue was filled with, in his opinion, a bunch of egghead scientists padding their egos with big words, each one "knowing" the answers but all the answers were different.

Bill took a deep breath to calm down, stretched his neck in all directions, and uttered a curse when he banged his knee recrossing his legs in the cramped quarters. The President's voice penetrated his thoughts.

"… experiencing phenomena that, although measured scientifically, cannot be explained easily and is causing widespread concern. We do know that what has been and is now occurring—the geographic upheavals, massive storms, changing weather patterns—will continue to affect us throughout the world. Earth, and the space around it, is undergoing severe unrest. So in order to prepare you for the possible ramifications and to alleviate anxieties, I've asked a team of scientists to present information on this subject. Time is of the essence. We will go now to Los Angeles and the Chairman of the …"

"Here they come," Bill hissed at his production team.

The director's voice boomed over the headset. "Stand by, audio. Ready, camera one. In four, three, two, one. Take it—cue him!"

They were up. It looked okay, Bill thought, wiping his forehead on his sleeve.

"… difficult to admit we don't have all the answers. Our first speaker, Dr. Roy Donahue, will present some background information on …"

Bill's throat felt like it was closing when he saw a glitch on the screen caused by another power hit. "Jesus Christ," he muttered and glared at the engineer, who merely shrugged. Some things just couldn't be explained.

Bill had to ignore the speech and focus his attention on the monitors and his own responsibilities. The next introduction caught his attention and he tuned back in.

"… internationally known author and lecturer, Dr. Dwight Atwood has had professional careers in the earth sciences, aerospace, and computer industries, and has integrated his knowledge into the—ah—spiritual realm. He has been called a psychic. In this time of crisis, the administration will remain open to all possible avenues of enlightenment. We are hoping Dr. Atwood can shed some light on what appears to be a universe going haywire. Dr. Atwood?" A slight smirk tweaked the corner of Donahue's mouth as polite applause accompanied Atwood to the podium.

Interesting intro, Bill thought. The poor guy faced an uphill battle for credibility, at least in present company, but the name was familiar. In fact, he was sure his mother, Julie, had given him some of Atwood's books to read.

What really drew Bill's attention to Atwood was his face. Deep lines ran from his nose to the corners of his mouth, reminding Bill of a Native American. His shoulder-length gray hair added to the image. The timbre in Atwood's voice had the sound engineer making a few hasty adjustments on the audio board.

"Mr. President. Ladies and gentlemen. I am honored to be asked to discuss the photon phenomenon occurring at this time in history. There are no known precedents for the recent events. Our Earth is nearing the completion of a cycle initiated nearly two hundred thousand years ago. The ancient ones called it "The Shift of the Ages." I will present my theories in laymen's terms and urge you to be aware of the seriousness and time frame of the possible—and probable—result of Earth's changing vibrations."

Power hits interrupted the signal more frequently and the air turned blue with four-letter words blasting through headsets. "We can't find the damn problem!" Bill said to the Washington producer, who didn't buy it. "We've triple checked everything.

There's no logical reason for this to be happening." Bill wished to hell he were somewhere, anywhere, else.

"… intensity of the planet's magnetic field, a forerunner of polar reversals, has decreased due to the slowing of Earth's rotation. At the same time, the rate of fundamental vibration, the Earth's heartbeat, has increased from the standard eight hertz to thirteen. This fluctuation is significant in that Earth's vibration rate affects our own. Each holographically tuned cell within our bodies is attempting to match this vibration. In other words, we and our Earth are being transformed."

The audience erupted with questions as Atwood paused to scan audience reaction with an intensity that made Bill's heart beat faster. "We are spiritual beings living in physical bodies. As such, those people who are ready spiritually will shift to a higher frequency. It will be accomplished through awakening to unconditional love and compassion. We must let go of fear! I ask—no, I pray—that you keep an open mind. It is imperative. The Zero Point of the Shift is upon us—perhaps a month away, or a week. Possibly hours. For the sake of mankind, I implore you to become aware." Atwood's knuckles whitened as he gripped the sides of the podium.

Bill shivered. This was the kind of stuff his mother talked about. Atwood was passionate, yes, but what made him think all this stuff was imminent? What's he know that he's not telling, Bill wondered.

He glanced at the monitors and swore under his breath at the unsteady waves drifting across the screen. He glared at Tex, who was frantically pushing buttons and turning dials, his face sweaty. What the hell is going on, he thought.

"... only those materials that resonate with the Earth will survive the coming disruption. Is plastic resonant? Rubber? We've already experienced severe power failures. Will fuels survive the Shift? I ask you to consider what the future holds ...."

Everyone's attention was riveted on Atwood. Bill heard, "Oh, my God!" and "That's bullshit!" through his headset.

The audience peppered Atwood with questions as phrases from his lecture caught and stuck in Bill's mind. We're in something called Photon energy—it's getting very close to a peak—the potential magnitude could be—will be—overwhelming. Bill felt hot and cold, wanting to not believe, but knowing deep down that he was hearing the truth.

Bill thought of Kathy, his wife, and their two children. Joey and Erica were growing up while he was on the damn road. He knew the traveling put a strain on his marriage but what the hell could he do about it? It took money to eat and this was the best way he knew to make it. His eyes stung with unshed tears as a wave of longing swept through him. He wondered if Kathy was watching the broadcast and, if so, how she felt about it.

Atwood leaned forward and, taking a deep breath, lowered his voice and spoke with intensity. "Ladies and gentlemen. To the degree that you can trust in a Higher Power, release fear and judgment, and love unconditionally; to that degree you will be prepared to survive the coming Shift emotionally, physically, and spiritually."

Bill clenched his fists as he struggled to comprehend the warning, "... broadcast technologies will be unable to function ...."

Bill and Tex glanced at each other, then at the wall of electronic video equipment. It was impossible to imagine the chaotic ramification if Atwood was speaking the truth.

Atwood spoke of physical sensations many people had been experiencing for the past year. "… flu-like symptoms, including aches and nausea, forgetfulness, fatigue, tension and unreasonable anxiety, vivid and meaningful dreams. Time seems to pass more quickly than it used to. Events seem to be speeding up due to the body's attempt to match the rapid pulsations of Earth's vibration. This and more will …"

All heads were nodding, including the President's. At the moment, Bill's symptoms were worse than ever. He knew exactly what Atwood was talking about.

"What will it be like after this so-called Shift?" someone asked, voicing everyone's thoughts.

"I can only speculate. Some people will remain in the dense Third Dimension until—and if—they're ready to ascend to the Fifth Dimension. Those who have grown spiritually will shift to a higher frequency. Those who have developed a complete trust in the God Force will ascend. They will experience a different kind of life, one filled with peace and love. It will not include those left behind."

Bill recalled that for the past few years, every other movie had seemed to be about shifts in consciousness or dimensions. The same for sci-fi television programs. We're being prepared for something, Bill thought. Some people will go and others will stay. What if Kathy and the kids do this thing and I don't? Or what if none of us—what—ascend? What if we're left in a world filled with war and fear and disease? A wave of panic swept through Bill.

At that moment the furniture, the lights—the entire building—began to shake. Screams of "Earthquake!" filled the room as glass shattered and cameras fell to the floor. People dove under the large conference table or headed for doorways, falling over chairs and each other. The noise was horrendous. Blackness filled the room.

Bill watched in terror as the equipment console fell to the floor tearing out cables and power lines.

"Oh God, it's happening. It's really happening!"

PART ONE

Winds of Change

In the beginning God created the heaven and the earth. And the earth was without form and void; and darkness was upon the face of the deep. And the Spirit of God moved upon the face of the waters.

And God said, "Let there be light," and there was light. And God called the light Day and the darkness He called Night. And the evening and morning were the first day.

And God said, "Let there be a firmament in the midst of the waters, and let it divide the waters from the waters." And God made the firmament, and divided the waters which were under the firmament from the waters which were above the firmament: and it was so.

And God called the firmament Heaven. And the evening and the morning were the second day. And God said, "Let the waters under the heaven be gathered together unto one place, and let the dry land appear," and it was so.

And God called the dry land Earth; and the gathering together of the waters called He Seas: and God saw that it was good.

From the Book of Genesis

Chapter One

The telephone jarred Julie out of her visionary journey. She quickly unwound her long legs from her yoga position, feet tripping on the faded cushion tucked into her warm niche on the deck, and raced to answer it. The effort made her dizzy but she was getting used to that.

"I got your message about the Shift," Kathy said when Julie answered the phone. Her voice was unsteady. "I feel it, too, Julie. My whole body seems to be vibrating. The car's packed, the kids are ready, and we're coming to stay with you in Takoma Springs. Bill's in L.A. again, working on some damn TV special, but I left a message on his voice mail that I'm leaving for Colorado right now."

"Kathy, slow down for heaven's sake. Take a deep breath and relax. You won't do Joey and Erica any good if you're out of control. You'll scare them half to death."

Kathy was intuitive. She didn't need anyone to tell her it was time to leave Phoenix. "Yes, yes, I know." She took a deep breath. "I'm okay now. You know what's kind of strange, Julie? It's Joey. He's so quiet. That's weird in itself, but he keeps patting me on the back, saying everything will be okay. He doesn't even know what's happening."

"He's clairvoyant, Kathy. Amazingly so for a five-year-old. You've known that since he first started talking. In many respects,

I'll bet he knows more than we do. Whatever his destiny is for this lifetime, I'm sure it's important. His angels are watching over him, as well as Erica and you and Bill. None of us are alone on this journey, honey."

"Oh, I know, Julie," Kathy sighed. "Thanks. Thanks for being there for us."

The sincerity in her daughter-in-law's voice brought tears to Julie's eyes. They had come a long way, she and Kathy, and she was grateful for the close and honest friendship they had shared throughout the years.

Tall, blonde and beautiful, Kathy had the patience of Job when it came to her children, and she needed every ounce of it. She'd had a career as a model before she was married but had put aside her own aspirations to be a full-time mother. Most of the time, she loved it. But then, none of us are saints, Julie thought. Their friendship was more than an in-law relationship. Kathy was adopted and never knew her birth family's background. Her adoptive parents, while warm and loving, had died young, and her lonely struggle made her doubly appreciative of Julie and Dave's family. Julie was grateful for this woman she loved as her own.

"My prayers will be with you and the kids every inch of the way," Julie reassured her. "Who knows what it's really going to be like. I'll feel better with you guys here, where I can see you and touch you. Be sure to carry plenty of water and blankets. And don't forget the cell phone, okay?"

"Got it. We're out the door even as we speak. And, please, don't worry about us. We'll be fine. We love you."

"I love you all, too. Drive carefully. I'll be waiting."

~ ~ ~

Julie hung up the phone and a tremor of apprehension swept through her. She broke out in a cold sweat. Was it knowing that Kathy faced a long trip alone with two small children, and time was short? Or was something else wrong? Julie shivered.

Beautiful blue-eyed Joey, with his bone-straight honey-colored hair, irrepressible good nature and boundless energy, would be okay. But she wondered whether little Erica, just a year old, had the ability to sit still in a car seat for more than half an hour. Erica was a charmer, an angel with a button-nose, sparkly blue eyes, and soft brown curls framing delicate features. She already knew how to twist her daddy around her tiny finger. Thank God they were coming.

Julie supposed it could be called a shift in realities, a major one. The changes in the universe that had begun a couple of years ago were now affecting everyone on planet Earth—and probably some who weren't. The Photon energy. The Zero Point. It defies human understanding and challenges the very ground we walk on, she thought. Besides, we've already faced so many challenges, dealt with so many lost loved ones. Why do we need to go through another major change, for Pete's sake?

A Photon phenomenon had enveloped the universe 26,000 years ago, with devastating results. It would turn the world upside down once again, although she hoped not literally, as some prophets predicted. It was hailed as Armageddon, the Tribulation and the Ascension. Quotes from Nostradamus, Edgar Cayce and The Book of Revelation were used to try to explain it. God was playing with Mother Earth's heartbeat, raising her vibration, changing her magnetic field. Who knew what the results would be? Speculation only succeeded in feeding overwhelming fear, but Julie was certain that love, awareness, and trust were the keys to survival.

She put a kettle of water on for tea and gazed out the window, looking at but not seeing the fields and forest. Personal shifts could be just as life changing. She remembered her first traumatic life change based on very earthly experiences, her life during her first 40 years, the loneliness, and life following her divorce from Ray. Despite the pain, the separation had been a glorious awakening, the first major step on her spiritual growth path. Julie had come alive. She discovered her creative talents and received credit and kudos for her work as a writer. And, much to her delight, she found she was still attractive to the opposite sex. Life was good and everything that had happened to her since then had been a build up, a preparation, for the events that would, she felt, culminate within a matter of days. Her heart skipped a beat but she vowed not to go into fear.

She wondered if those without a clue about cataclysmic events in motion were better off. They'll handle it or not, she decided, or maybe just leave the planet. It was their choice. For some reason she'd been forewarned and, hopefully, forearmed. As much to reassure herself as anything else, she took a deep breath, raised her head toward the heavens, and said, "Okay, God, I'm ready when you are." Biting her lip she added, "Almost."

The kettle's high-pitched whistle drew her out of her reverie.

A cup of hot cinnamon and apple tea warming her hands, she went out to the deck. The sun had risen an hour ago but it was still cold in the shadows. She sat cross-legged on the old comfortable cushion, resting her back against the warm cedar siding.

The old fleece sweatshirt, well-worn jeans, and the sun on her face felt warm and soothing. She brushed her slightly graying hair off her face, leaned her head against the wall, and took in the beauty of the pines and aspens. Hard-earned wrinkles softened. Julie breathed deeply. Early morning forest and meadow flowers perfumed the air. A meadowlark broke the stillness with his song and a hawk circled high above. In the distance she heard the crunch of tires on the dirt road and watched a small cloud of dust slowly dissipate in the gentle breeze.

Wind Dancer Ranch, Dave's and her dream come true, was situated in the majestic Colorado Rockies. The cedar mountain home was nestled against the dark green pines and looked out on rich pasture land. Their choice of deep teal green carpeting, cranberry red accents, and rich plaids made their open and spacious home warm and welcoming. Large windows filled the A-frame prow and brought the outdoors in, providing fantastic views of the jagged mountains.

She met Dave two years after her divorce and both knew right away that they were soulmates. Her husband was tall and handsome; his ruddy complexion, chiseled features and graying hair gave him a distinguished look. His soft brown eyes could melt her heart in a flash, and his hugs were warm and given freely.

They had found Takoma Springs by accident and had fallen in love with it immediately. It was peaceful and friendly, a small town with a big heart. They soon realized it was not accidental. It was karmic. This was where they needed to be to carry out their soul contract. The piece of land that called to them was familiar on a deep level. Psychics later told them that Julie had lived there eons ago and had been responsible for taking her soul group through an ascension. Apparently she had made a commitment to do it again.

And then there was Crystal Mountain, her firm anchor in this unstable world. It literally glowed in the distance, its warm golden aura and magnificent pyramid shape setting it apart from the others. She often wondered what secrets it held, for it seemed to radiate mysterious vibrations for those who tuned in. Its powerful protection wrapped itself around Julie. It was inconceivable that anything could disrupt the perfection of this day, her life, her world, her universe. But "it" was coming—and soon. She shuddered at the thought and acknowledged the need to ground herself, get centered, regroup, and reflect on what had brought her to this point in her life. It might be her last chance for a long time. A relaxing meditation would help her enormously.

Taking three deep breaths, she sank deeper and deeper into her consciousness. Slowly counting from ten down to one, focusing on her breath, she visualized roots growing from her feet deep into and blending with the golden warmth of Mother Earth's womb. She felt herself let go, releasing tension in mind and body.

Filling herself with white light, she offered a prayer of thanks for the blessings in her life and asked for divine protection and guidance. Incessant mind chatter, distracting repetition of the same thoughts over and over again, slowly ceased and she entered the Silence.

Julie found herself walking through a beautiful meadow, a gentle breeze caressing her face. She smelled the wild flowers and heard birds singing as if they were real. A tall handsome young man with warm blue eyes materialized in the path ahead, a beautiful smile spreading across his face as he stepped closer. "Hello, Mom."

"What—who are you?"

"You knew me twenty-five years ago—when I was a baby."

"Oh, my God," Julie said, barely able to breathe. "Danny. My beautiful baby, Danny."

"Yes, Mom, it's me. I chose to appear to you as you see me now rather than as a baby, since babies have a somewhat limited vocabulary," he smiled.

"Oh, Danny, how I've missed you. It was so hard when you left. The Spina Bifida made you so sick and you were in such pain. I know now it was meant to be, but I didn't know it then."

"It was our agreement, our contract. I wasn't in anywhere near as much pain as you were. I had to help you open up to your emotions, to face what was missing in your life. And you helped me fulfill past-life karma, too."

"Well, you certainly succeeded and gave me a strength I didn't know I had."

"That's why I've come to you today. You do have incredible strength. Remember that because you'll need it. Our time together is not over, Mom. We still have much to teach each other."

Julie's child began to fade. He raised his hand in farewell. His smile lingered as he disappeared in a soft cloud.

"Danny! Don't go," she said, longing in her voice. It had been so many years since she'd been in touch with him. An immense love filled her heart.

Julie returned from her deep meditation, slowly becoming aware of her surroundings. "Thank you, dearest Danny, for everything," she whispered. He had brought her the gift of life, his and hers, and she would be eternally grateful.

Chapter Two

Julie had warned her family about the coming Shift, but Kathy was the only one she'd heard from. Julie could enlighten them but they had to make their own decision on how to deal with it. Dave understood her. He even understood her when her words came out backwards and upside down. During their fifteen years of marriage they had both learned to take her premonitions seriously.

She called him on his cell phone in Los Angeles. Voices hummed in the background.

"Dave, it's coming. The Shift is really going to happen and soon. I know it. I sense it. You've got to get home right away. I want to be with you—and the family."

"I have to finish up in L.A.," he said. "We're wrapping up the meeting now. I'll catch the flight to Albuquerque right after. It'll take five hours to drive from there. Hang in there, babe. I'll be there before you know it. Please don't worry, Julie."

"Hurry, Dave. I need you. I love you."

"Me, too, babe."

Damn it, why couldn't he leave immediately? What if there weren't any flights out of L.A.? What if the planes were full? What if, what if, what if? Julie had to face the fact that she was scared—anticipating the future, but human and scared.

She gave Max, their German shepard, a loving scratch behind his ears and went to the basement to check the water supply. She had stored enough survival water to last several people for a few weeks. She trusted the universe to provide, but her own efforts gave her a sense of control and security.

Julie added a few drops of colloidal silver to each bottle of water, checked the supply of candles and matches, the shelves of canned and dried foods, the wool and cotton blankets, toilet paper, soap and first aid supplies.

Looking at the stored goods, she recalled the first time she had collected survival items. In the sixties the atom bomb scare had taken hold and bomb shelters appeared in back yards. She had prepared a corner of the basement with food and water but fortunately fears eased and shelters disappeared. She had jumped through even bigger hoops in California, anticipating The Big One. That had been an enormous fear for her, irrational and out of proportion to reality, or so she thought. She and Dave moved to Colorado and missed the 8.5 quake and the resulting damage and loss of life.

Now she had to prepare once again. It would be different this time. Much, much different. The phone startled her. She ran up the basement stairs, dropped the receiver on the counter and finally gasped, "Hello?"

"Mom, are you okay?" Blessed Jon. Her son had been her emotional glue from the time he could talk. Such an old soul.

"I'm fine. Really, I am," she said, catching her breath. "I just forget I'm not twenty-five anymore with the legs of a gazelle. I'm so glad you called. How are you, Jon?"

"Doing great," he laughed. "And you will never be old, Mom. But fill me in. I got your message and have been feeling real strange myself. Is it what I think it is?"

"Yeah. That's what I'm getting. And soon. Where are you?"

"At home. Just got back from the lecture tour. I had planned on getting some shut-eye. Maybe this isn't the time."

Julie's heart pounded. Home meant San Francisco. "Maybe not. Oh, Jon, I just don't know. Your angels will be with you wherever you are but if there's any way you can get here, I think they'd be overjoyed. But not nearly as much as I would be." She paused. "There may not be much time."

"I hear ya, Mom. But, hey, hang loose, okay? You know I'll be with you whether I'm there or not. You'll do great and so will I. Mom, the other line's ringing. I gotta go."

"Okay, honey. Stay in touch, okay?"

"Of course I will. Talk to you later. Love ya."

The line went dead.

Julie sighed. Jon never planned more than half an hour ahead. That was part of his charm. Tall, with deep-set blue eyes and a gorgeous smile, he was a Brad Pitt look-alike. He loved the opposite sex and they loved him. His off-the-wall sense of humor had pulled her through difficult times more than once, making her laugh even when she didn't want to. He was a good writer and an even better speaker. He used his innate sense of humor to get his point across. At age of thirty, Jon had a mind of his own. All she could offer was information. She couldn't direct his life.

Her body prickled suddenly. She sat down as a dizzy spell and a slight wave of nausea swept over her. Vibrational changes were taking place in her body with a lot more frequency lately. It would pass. The spells didn't frighten her anymore; they merely made her temporarily uncomfortable. Her body tingled and she felt slightly out of control, certainly one of the more difficult feelings for her to accept. After she'd discovered what it was, she relaxed a little. Trust. That's what it was all about.

The dizziness passed and Julie went to the mudroom. She tugged on old work boots, grabbed a warm jacket and her worn leather gloves, and started down the path to the barn. Faithful and devoted Max and the forever-smiling golden retriever, Sandy who, much to Max's chagrin, had joined them six months before, jumped at Julie's heels. Sometimes their boundless energy and single-minded desire to please was close to claustrophobic. But she appreciated their companionship, especially on those long, lonely evenings when Dave was gone. "Okay, okay! I love you, too," she laughed, reassuring them with quick hugs.

The path was muddy, thanks to a sprinkler head gone amuck, but she didn't mind. Her boots could come off at the back door. She'd never gotten around to getting some for her canine companions. Julie smiled at the thought of eight little boots lined up beside hers.

The barn was warm and rich with animal smells and sounds. Misty, her beautiful bay, 15 hands high and proud of it, snorted and whinnied as Julie approached with a bucket of oats. The sweet-tempered horse gave her a soft, velvety kiss on the hand. Misty could run like the wind. Racing across the fields had always been an exhilarating experience for both of them.

Julie fed Dave's pinto, Orion—a magnificent animal of 16 hands and more horse than she could handle—and opened the stall doors so they could run through the tall grass in the fresh air, muscles rippling as they stretched their long legs.

The goats jammed up at the door, eager to chomp their way through as much grass as they could find. Daisy Mae's baby struggled on wobbly legs to keep up. The old barn cats were as mellow as ever, stretched out in their lazy fashion, but always on alert for any unlucky critters scurrying in the hay.

She scattered feed for the chickens and was rewarded with a couple of fresh eggs. After cleaning the stalls, Julie closed the big barn door, and trudged back to the house, revived by the activity.

The wind was stronger and the sun wasn't as warm as it had been earlier. It didn't feel right. Her heart beat faster. Beads of sweat broke out on her forehead in spite of the cold.

Julie's pine-paneled office with its extensive bookshelves was her lifeline to the world. She couldn't imagine life without her computer. How else would she be able to write, send e-mail, keep records, surf the Net? It was a necessary part of her career as a writer, but it was made of plastic. Would it soon be a pile of dust with whatever metal parts it held sitting on top of it?

Logging on, she found several e-mail messages, two from friends with premonitions like hers. She sensed fear in their words, so she replied with confirmation and encouragement. There was also an email from her stepson, Chris. He and his wife, Ellen, lived in Raleigh, North Carolina, but they remained close. They were young and vulnerable. But 28 wasn't young anymore; children had to grow up fast to survive these days.

Chris was in law enforcement. He was involved in investigations for the most part, but was called back to active duty when needed. He was good at it, compassionate and respected by his co-workers. Ellen had her own growing legal practice and dreaded every time Chris went on “hard core” duty as she called it. They respected Julie’s predictions but buying into the Photon energy was too much for them.

His note said they both had a touch of the flu but that they felt snug and safe in their home. Julie doubted if the flu was responsible for their discomfort. Lately there had been a strange energy around Ellen that really worried Julie. It was discomforting but Spirit hadn’t allowed her to check it out. When a karmic lesson is involved, it needed to be learned without outside help. All Julie could do was send her love.

She stood up and the unpleasant dizziness swept over her again. The waves were coming faster and faster.

Time. Now there was a concept that had been shattered. She didn’t need to be told that time was speeding up. Days and weeks flew by and she sometimes felt she was hanging on by her teeth. The list of uncompleted tasks grew. Time was folding in on itself. And yet the anomaly was that, because of so-called wrinkles in time, a drive that would have taken seven hours years ago still took seven hours. It was crazy-making. She had to admit the whole space/time continuum confused the hell out of her.

Julie absent-mindedly wandered from bookshelf to table, rearranging books and photographs. She picked up a photo of Dave smiling at her as only he could, and her heart skipped a beat. He could still do that to her after all these years. She slowly replaced it.

There had been a lot of speculation about this Zero Point, even in the Book of Revelation. Julie refused to buy into the doom and gloom prophecies. The transformation would be enough of a challenge.

Out of curiosity Julie turned on the TV. Enough new things would soon be happening in the atmosphere that scientists—and, no doubt, politicians—would be thrown into an absolute tizzy. The devastating disasters of the last few years made end-of-the-world tabloid headlines commonplace. It had been the same with UFO reports until their existence could no longer be denied. The government had done some fast talking to maintain a reasonable semblance of credibility in the face of major cover-up scandals.

Reception was poor and static filled the airwaves. "… in Los Angeles at ten twenty-three Pacific Standard Time. All communication has been cut off … more information as we receive … Repeat: a seven point five earthquake rocked the …"

"Oh, my God! Oh, no!" Julie cried. "Not now! This can't be happening! Dave! Bill! Where are you? Oh please, God, let them be all right!" Her heart raced and she gasped for breath as the news anchor plowed through the bad news.

"New York City … enormous power outage … investigating the cause and we'll … as long as our generators can handle the load. Now to Travis Cutler at Times Square … Can you hear me, Travis?"

Not well, based on Travis's reaction. The noise was deafening and people were running in all directions. The chaos would escalate. Interference on every channel was no doubt related to wild fluctuations in Earth's electromagnetic field. Radio would be in trouble, too. She had to know if her loved ones were okay, where they were, and whether there was any possible way to escape L.A.

Julie grabbed her cell phone and tried unsuccessfully to reach Dave. Frantic, she dialed her son, Steve, in Boulder. During military training a few years ago, he'd faced survival situations in the mountains fairly well. She had jokingly called him the Harrison Ford of the family. He looked a little like him, too. He answered on the fourth ring.

"Mom! I got your message but I couldn't get through to you. How are things in Takoma Springs?"

"Oh, Steve, there's been an earthquake in L.A. and both Dave and Bill are there! I'm so scared!"

"Calm down, Mom. They'll be fine. They both have a way of being in the right place at the right time."

"I know, but there's so much else happening right now."

"How bad was it?"

"A seven point five, from what I heard. The TV is full of static. What if they're hurt, Steve? What if they can't get out?"

"They're big boys, Mom. Survivors. I know you'll hear from them as soon as they can get through. How about Kathy? Does she know?"

"I don't know. She might have heard it on the car radio. Oh, Lord, I hope she didn't! She's heading here with the kids and that would really send her into a tailspin." Julie took a deep breath. There was absolutely nothing she could do about any of it. Better to change the subject.

"How are you guys doing? Are the boys okay?"

"I'm in the middle of preparing for our annual audit at work. I'm beginning to get dizzy just looking at figures. Megan's up to her ears between the boys and work. Jesse and Mike are fine but she's stressed to the max."

Steve and Megan were so conscientious and took life so seriously, Julie thought. When they'd been blessed with twins, she'd wondered if they would have the stamina to deal with them. They did, but what a learning experience it had been. The Shift was serious business, too, but given Steve's comments, she wasn't about to push her advice any further.

"I don't want to scare the family," Steve said, "so, you know, we're okay. I've got some extra food and water. The kids really miss you guys, so maybe we can get together soon."

"We miss all of you, too, Steve."

"We're going camping in the morning so don't worry about us. In fact, we might even get a head start and leave tonight."

"Camping?" Julie bit her lower lip. "That … sounds like fun. Just be careful. You know you're in my prayers and I love you very much. Don't ever forget that, ever. And give Mike and Jesse an extra big hug from Grandma."

"You bet, Mom. I love you, too. Let me know if you hear anything. And don't worry, okay?"

When Julie hung up the phone, she didn't know if the lump in her throat was for Dave and Bill or for Steve. He was so vulnerable. The ultimate peacemaker. He was still suffering from emotional fallout with his father. Julie was confident that Steve and his family were capable of handling themselves in the high country. They loved the wilderness; in fact, that could be a good place for them to be, close and well grounded to Mother Earth. It just wouldn't have been Julie's first choice.

Chapter Three

Julie paced from room to room. Fear of something she couldn't quite put her finger on nagged at her. It was above and beyond Dave and the kids, and very disorienting.

Writing always grounded her, kept her "on track," so she headed for her office. She'd been working on an autobiography of sorts, describing experiences she'd encountered on her spiritual path. It was a chronicle of events for her grandchildren that, depending on what happened in the next few days, weeks, and months, would help them understand what led up to the Shift.

Max and Sandy, tired of romping outdoors, padded along behind her. Settling herself in the dark blue swivel chair, as familiar and comfortable as an old shoe, she opened the file on the computer.

She had already covered Danny and her divorce from Ray. Then came her college degree at age 40 and for the first time in a long while, a sense of being someone. Some One. Not a wife, not the kids' mom, not someone for everyone else to take a piece of. She had given her energy and power away to all of them. Now she was Julie, television producer, a teacher, a free and independent woman.

"A new employee had arrived at the university," she wrote, fingers racing across the keyboard, "a stimulating, vibrant feminist named Marcy who turned my spiritual beliefs upside down. I was ready for it and my life changed totally and forever.

"Marcy introduced me to a psychic, a gentle man who used words I'd never heard before. He told me things that had happened in my life that no one knew but me. He touched on feelings I was experiencing but hadn't shared with anyone. How had he known those things? He told me of strange and unimaginable events that had occurred in my past lives, and then proceeded to share what he saw happening in my future. I didn't believe any of it and wanted to believe all of it. I didn't know what to believe. I went from skepticism about reincarnation to a full-blown believer as layers of doubt were replaced by waves of insight."

It was the beginning of an incredible spiritual journey, a search that was exciting, inspiring, loving, and definitely mind-boggling. With due diligence, she read everything she could find, attended workshops and seminars, searching for answers and understanding. Julie practiced meditation, slowly developing her own methods and beliefs.

"I had an intense desire to share my newfound realizations with the world," she continued, "but found that the world didn't want to know. My 'new' reality was one of feeling alone and in spiritual isolation. When Shirley MacLaine came out of the metaphysical closet with *Out on a Limb*, I wept with joy and relief. I wasn't alone on this crazy path."

Julie's fingers flew over the keyboard, pouring out feelings, fears, and thoughts. So much to say, so little time to say it.

The phone brought her back to reality with a jolt. Heart pounding, she grabbed the receiver.

"Jeannie! Oh, thank God! Where are you?"

"In Tucson. Oh, Julie, I'm so scared! You know I've always trusted you but this time I thought you'd flipped out, that you were really nuts. But something's happening. I feel weird and last night I had this scary dream and now it's all real. I know it, I feel it. I just heard about the earthquake in L.A. and Jerry and I want to come home. We want to be with you and Dad. Can we stay with you for a while?"

There was one thing about her stepdaughter, Jean: Her lips spoke only the truth. Petite and pretty, her delicate features belied a strength she didn't know she had. As a little sister to four brothers, she'd been forced to toughen up, to be able to say "back off" and make it stick. They were all very protective of her, a nice feeling but easily over done. Julie felt close to her; their relationship was grounded in past lives and the connection was strong.

"Of course you guys can stay here! You know there's always room. When can you leave? I don't think there's a lot of time, Jeannie." Julie tried to sound casual but Tucson was a long way away.

"Jerry thinks I'm crazy and blames it on the pregnancy but I told him we have to be on the road in half an hour or I'm leaving without him. I guess he believes me."

"I expect he does," smiled Julie. "Let's see. It's about a six hundred mile trip. That's a long stretch for someone eight months pregnant. Are you sure you can handle it?"

"I need to be home, Julie. I need to be with you guys."

"Okay, I understand. Just tell Jerry to take it easy. And, Jeannie, please keep an eye out for the old 4Runner. Kathy and the kids are on their way alone and I'm worried about them."

"I'm glad they're coming. Don't worry. We'll watch for them. What about Bill and Dad?"

Julie hesitated. No need to give Jean any more worries. "They'll be here. Be sure to take plenty of water with you. And Jeannie? Think about your baby and stay calm. We don't want any early deliveries! Trust your Guardian Angels. They're with you."

"Yeah, I will. And thanks. I needed that, Julie. I love you. Tell Dad I love him, too."

"See you soon, Jeannie. I love you."

She put the phone down slowly. Love was truly the ultimate and only thing that mattered in this crazy world. "Dear God," she prayed, "keep them all safe."

Three o'clock. Where had the day gone? She turned the TV on again, hoping for news, but the signal was poor. The whole world would be glued to their sets, absorbing panic as if they didn't have enough of their own. It wouldn't be long before the TV anchors announced that the end of the world was coming. Chances are they'd be off the air first. She'd have to depend on ESP for her information. TRUST. Breathe in trust, breathe out fear. Breathe in trust, breathe out fear.

The Photon energy. When she had first heard those words, it had sounded like science fiction. She'd made a smart-aleck comment, but had felt a fear deep inside, a subtle knowing it was the truth.

"Never accept the words of others," her teacher had said. "Take them inside, ask your own guides and see how it feels. If the shoe fits, wear it."

Well, it fit very well and she had eventually been able to tie up the laces. She accepted the inevitable and prayed for guidance on how to carry on from there. She didn't go out and push the information on friends and family unless they showed an interest.

Tabloids lapped up the bizarre predictions and the psychic networks made a fortune. The mainstream population was in denial; very few were ready to hear it. But the weather and earth changes could not be denied. Massive disasters around the world—earthquakes, floods, volcanoes, Florida's changing coastline—triggered a demand for answers. The 300 mph winds across Europe were devastating, and 9.5 earthquakes had caused incredible fires in Iran and Iraq. The Pacific Rim, the rim of fire, had suffered explosive volcanoes, setting off monstrous tsunamis. Thick volcanic ash saturated the atmosphere, and planes were forced out of the sky. Only emergency flights had been allowed.

Meteor showers cast fireballs from the UK across France, Spain and Germany. Escalating disease and violence in cities frightened an already-scared population. Ever so slowly the doors began to open for sharing and preparing. So many thousands had lost their lives from worldwide disasters and plagues. She had said many prayers for the lost souls, had cried until she had run out of tears.

The volcano at Mammoth Lakes in California blew six months ago, followed by the earthquake that jolted Nevada, Utah, and Wyoming. Most were caught by surprise. The big L.A. earthquake was a wake-up call for San Franciscans. Thousands of northern Californians had sought safer areas and tent cities sprang up in the desert. Some people remained in their homes, in denial; still others accepted the inevitable and chose to remain anyway.

That had been her youngest son, Jon's, decision. But the city lived in fear and rightfully so; two months after the LA quake, northern California was shaken to its foundations.

Steve and his family, along with Jon, had been in Sacramento visiting their father when the San Francisco earthquake hit. They'd been tossed around and the city sustained a lot of damage but the boys had survived. Their father, however, had suffered a massive heart attack. Ray's death had been tough on the boys, but Jon and Bill had pretty much made their peace with him beforehand. Steve hadn't.

Scientists finally admitted that the massive solar flares had helped create the severe weather patterns experienced the last few years. They had caused power surges and outages and shifted the magma in the earth's core. Thanks to stray asteroids, people no longer wished upon a shooting star, except to perhaps never see one again.

And now the grand finale was on a collision course with Mother Earth. There was no stopping it now. Scientists predicted the world might implode because they simply had no way of measuring what was occurring. They didn't understand that it was a beginning, not an ending.

There was a time when enlightened consciousness ameliorated some of the Earth's unrest but now it was too late. The die was cast. Julie had to be true to her truth, helping awaken those who were open to it. She really wasn't a "woo-woo" type person, although she felt pretty "woo-woo" at the moment. She hoped someone would arrive soon.

Despite a lack of appetite, Julie lathered bread with peanut butter and found a soda in the fridge. She headed back to her spot on the deck, her corner of the world where she could hear the crickets and birds. There were a few chirps here and there but it was becoming strangely still, their cheerful songs almost muted except for the creaking branches of the old oak tree. Were animals and insects aware? Did they feel something happening?

Julie's pants were incredibly tight. What had caused all the bloating? Her Nikes felt two sizes too small.

Then she remembered the predictions. The body was redesigning itself to survive by recharging with extra water like a battery in order to contain the extensive electromagnetic changes. That recollection brought Julie to attention, the peanut butter sandwich forgotten. There was no doubt about it: The six-day transition had begun! She was painfully aware that those trying to get home to the safety of her nest might not make it in time. Blood drained from her face.

"Dear Lord," she implored, beginning the slide into fear. "Please, watch over my babies and bring Dave home safely. I really don't want to go through this alone." The lump in her throat threatened to erupt. She grabbed the cell phone on the first ring.

"I'm okay, babe." He was out of breath. "It was a good shaker but I was already close to the airport. I'm just a bit jittery."

Julie was in tears. "Oh, honey, I've been so scared. Thank God you're all right."

"I'm getting on a plane now. I don't know if it'll take off or not so keep your fingers crossed. The airport is an absolute zoo, everybody running everywhere! They're terrified by the earthquake, by whatever is going on in the ethers. I'm feeling really weird myself. My body feels like it's vibrating. It's two and a half hours to Albuquerque and then a long drive home, and I can't wait to get there!"

"Me too, honey."

"Stay in touch with me, Julie—you know, the way we do without phones."

"I will. Bill is down there somewhere, too. I'll try to tune in to you both. I've been so upset I forgot to even try. Oh, Dave, I love you so very much."

"I love you, too, babe." His voice was filled with emotion. The cell connection crackled.

"Dave? Dave!" The line was dead.

It wasn't fear so much as the anxiety of facing the unknown. Experiencing something that hadn't occurred in 26,000 years, for God's sake, was a bit overwhelming. Lighten up, Julie, she scolded herself. Dave is alive. That's all that matters right now.

She re-settled into a comfortable position once again. Closing her eyes, she relaxed her body as much as the bloat allowed. Deepening her meditation, she went into a state of peace and connection with her higher consciousness, her angels and guides. In her mind, her third eye, she brought her children forward, one by one, sending peace, confidence and love, knowing it would reach them on some level.

Kathy appeared in her vision. The 4Runner was tearing up the freeway.

"Mommy, don't drive so fast!" Joey scolded. "We'll get to Grandma's, I know we will. You're scaring me, Mommy!"

Kathy had a death grip on the wheel. Her cheeks were flushed, eyes glued to the freeway. She tried to sound calm. "It's okay. I'm okay. Is Erica still asleep?"

"She's waking up. I think she did something. She smells awful!"

"We'll stop soon, Joey. Hang in there. We've got to make all the headway we can. Jesus!" she cried as a car shot by her. "He must be doing at least 100 miles an hour! People are nuts out here!"

She had a surrealistic sensation of crawling in slow motion, moving against an ocean tide or a sea of mud. The damn seat belt was too tight around her middle. Maybe she should have just stayed in Phoenix. Was she insane? Her gut said no. The support of family was mandatory for this event. Besides, cities were not the place to be.

She noticed the gas gauge was close to empty just as a small whimper escaped from the mound of blankets in the car seat next to Joey. At the next exit, she pulled off the highway and found a line of ten cars leading to the only gas station. She'd never get there at this rate.

Kathy pulled in behind a travel trailer to wait her turn. Resting her head on the steering wheel, she closed her eyes and thought about Bill. They'd been through so much together. It was hard to live with him sometimes, but she couldn't live without him. Joey needed him and little Erica was so young she hardly knew him yet.

Kathy had held together pretty well until she heard about the earthquake on the radio. Was the building he was in safe? What floor had he been on? Was he hurt? Was he alive? Please let him be all right, please, please, God. Tears slid down her cheeks.

"Mommy, don't cry. I want Daddy, too, and I know he's okay. He'll find us at Grandma's, Mommy. Please don't cry," Joey begged.

Her son's plea brought Kathy back to her present predicament. His clairvoyant abilities never failed to amaze her. He'd known that their second child would be a girl. He had predicted Bill would get the job he'd just interviewed for. He even announced the start date.

From the time he could talk, Joey "knew" things. He could read minds and raising him was a challenge. Kathy wondered what his purpose in life was. It had to be something special.

She brushed the tears from her eyes. "I'm okay, Joey. Just frustrated. I know in my heart Daddy's safe. We'll all be at Gram's house soon and we'll get great big hugs, okay?"

"I know, Mommy. And I won't cry, either," he reassured her, although his blue eyes betrayed him.

Joey affected a fake smile for her benefit and Kathy had to laugh. Laughter was good. Bill would be fine and was probably as frantic as she was to be together again. They'd both make it somehow.

She closed her eyes and felt the connection with Julie in a way they had done so many times over the past few years. "If you believe it, you can achieve it," Julie always said. Kathy had been pretty skeptical at first, but trust had grown and there was a deep love between the two women.

A vision of Julie began to form in her mind, so real, Kathy suddenly felt at peace. She took a deep breath and her heartbeat slowed. A smile played with her lips. Her angels were with her, and with the children and Bill, too. Hadn't she seen enough signs of that in the last few years?

After a quiet thank you to her unseen support team, she moved the car up a couple of spaces and crawled into the back seat. Time for a quick diaper change and a snack for the baby. Thank God she was still nursing. She and Joey needed a potty break, too. Maybe everybody could use a snack, something to stop this strange tingling in her body, this feeling of disorientation.

Chapter Four

Joey had been right about one thing: His father was indeed frantic. Bill crawled his way out of the shaken high rise, helping as many as he could on the way down. Sirens screamed and the air was clogged with dust. His rental car was badly dented but functional.

Traffic was close to a standstill in L.A. Everyone wanted to get somewhere but they didn't know which direction to go. Many streets were blocked with debris and emergency crews. After much weaving and side street maneuvering, he was stuck on the 405, the great freeway parking lot, as Dave called it. Bill claimed cell phones had been invented simply to keep L.A. drivers from going nuts. But even those weren't working now and drivers were definitely reacting.

"I've got to get to the airport, damn it!" Bill shouted, leaning on the horn in frustration. His gut told him Kathy would try to reach his mother. Dave would try to get to Albuquerque, the closest airport to Takoma Springs, probably on United since he had a passion for collecting flier mileage for family vacations.

Bill smiled, remembering how close the blended family had been from the very beginning. Their fun times together cemented the love and support even deeper.

"Well, this isn't getting me anywhere. I'm out of here!" Disgusted, he grabbed his briefcase, slammed the car door and left it in the third lane of the four-lane freeway. He was lucky to have made it as far as he did. Drivers staying with their vehicles could be there for weeks.

Bill wove his way through the stalled vehicles, finally making it to the side of the road. With his tie and leather belt, he made his briefcase into a backpack and began jogging in the general direction of the airport. If he was going to die, it damn well wasn't going to happen while stuck on a frigging freeway.

He wished he'd worn his running shoes. Between the quake and the warnings from that Atwood guy, there was no doubt it was time to be with his family. They would all need each other.

Adrenaline coursed through his body as his wife and children filled his thoughts. He picked up speed and began chanting, "I can, I can, I know I can!" and like the little engine that could, Bill kept going.

Dave settled into the cramped seat of the United jet, more than ready to get the hell off the ground. It was packed and the tension was palpable. Someone must have been watching over him when the quake hit. He'd been enjoying the easy walk from the hotel conference room when the ground went ballistic. At least he'd been in an open area. He'd been thrown about some, but bruises would heal.

There was more fear than serious injuries in the terminal. He had stopped to help an elderly couple find a place to sit and rest, but they waved him on. He was damned fortunate his plane was at the gate. He hoped the pilot had every intention of taking off. The intercom interrupted his thoughts.

"This is your captain speaking. We've been delayed for take off due to more air traffic than we expected. We'll try to make you comfortable, and we'll let you know when we've been cleared for departure."

That was bad news. Time was of the essence.

Dave and the other passengers weren't aware of the strange things happening in the control tower, the unexplained blips on the screens, interference on headsets, confusion and rising panic. There was gridlock on the runways, confusion in the sky, and communication was non-existent.

Dave closed his eyes and tried to relax. He was reasonably calm, considering. A baby's cry reminded him of Julie's instructions to visually spread purple light throughout the plane to reduce tension and transmute negative energy. He did it, amazed at how it worked.

His thoughts turned to Julie. What an incredible gift she had been to him. He loved her more than he could say. She was his reason for living. Soulmates. Definitely the glue that held the whole family together, he thought. It still amazed him how two people could be so close. Even after 15 years he still got the same initial thrill when he held her in his arms or even when he thought of her. Please God, watch over her, he prayed silently. Help me get there quickly. Keep us all safe—our kids, everyone.

The dizziness came and went. He hoped it wasn't the flu. Deep down he knew better.

Julie shifted slightly and came up from the depths of her meditation. It had been deep; she had connected with some of her family. "So far, so good," she sighed. At least they were partially prepared, thanks to her relentless dissemination of information.

As excited as Julie was about meeting the new dimension, she was extremely anxious about the process of getting there. Just because she wasn't afraid of death per se, she didn't want to have to deal with the discomfort leading up to it. She felt the same way about the Shift.

Julie sipped her water, took a deep breath, and relaxed once again. Blocking out the world and extraneous thoughts, she focused her attention on Jean, bringing her image to her third eye, asking to connect with her energy.

"Jerry, for God's sake, I want to get home in one piece! Slow down … please!"

"Relax, Jeannie. Back off and go to sleep. I know how to drive."

"I'm sorry. I'm just scared. I've never felt weird like this before. Besides, we're too young. We haven't lived yet. I don't want to die, not on the freeway, not ever!" She took a deep breath. "I just love you so much." A tear escaped down her cheek.

"Yeah, I love you, too, kid. We'll make it, so quit worrying, okay?"

"Okay. I'll be all right. At least we've got each other and our baby."

"Right on, Jeannie. Keep that thought."

As if in agreement, the baby pushed gently against her rib cage. Eight months pregnant. They had wanted to wait before starting a family but that was not to be. A little spirit out there had been incredibly persistent, not to mention sneaky. Everything happens for a reason, so she and Jerry were relieved when the Baby Decision was taken out of their hands. Going to Tucson for his project was really more than she should have taken on just now, but pregnant for the first time, she had just wanted to be near her husband. She willed herself to relax and think positive thoughts for her own sake as well as the child's. She caressed her tummy as the baby stretched in the confined womb. Her thoughts focused on Wind Dancer Ranch.

"You know, I don't know why, but I just saw a picture of Julie curled up on her deck with the dogs and they looked so peaceful and strong." She smiled tentatively. "I think I really do feel better."

She awkwardly settled into the truck seat and wrapped herself in a blanket. "Someone should come up with seat belts for pregnant women," she grumbled. "Jerry, in case I fall asleep—which is highly unlikely at this point—don't forget to keep an eye out for Kathy and the kids. They're in the old 4Runner."

Jerry glanced at his wife and relaxed a bit, too. "I will, Jeannie."

~ ~ ~

Julie smiled. They were all right. Anxious, yes, but when Jerry put his mind on something, little could get him off track. God willing, they'll get here in time. Going through the Shift was better with family support, especially when no one knew for sure just what would happen. Even more so when you're very pregnant, Julie thought.

She was concerned that Jerry didn't really believe the warnings of the Shift, that he was merely going along to humor Jean. Maybe Dave, assuming he gets out of L.A. in time, could convince him how imperative it is to have faith in a Higher Power to help him get through this thing. Jerry thought Julie was way off the wall. Perhaps she was.

Julie released a deep sigh and shook off the uneasiness. Time to plug into Jon, her light-hearted, irrepressible youngest son. Was he high and dry in the hills of San Francisco, or might he possibly find his way to Wind Dancer Ranch, too?

With the thought of him, Jon's image emerged through a misty haze in her mind's eye. Bless his heart; he was smiling. The communication was non-verbal but as real as talking out loud.

"Yes, Mom, I'm smiling at you. It's getting easier and easier to stay tuned in to you. There you are, cozy on the deck, checking on your chicks just like a mother hen," he teased.

"Jon Cramer! Just how long have you been eavesdropping on my subconscious?"

"Long enough to make sure you were okay, Mom. Don't worry. I won't go where I don't belong. I felt you coming my way and beat you to it. What's the haps, Mom? Is everyone okay? Are you alone?"

She had to admit that this astral contact was amazing. Neither of them understood how it worked but it didn't matter. No long distance phone bill for them.

"Yes, I'm alone. But don't worry, I've got the pups and Dave is on his way, I think. L.A.'s a mess but he survived the earthquake. He's safe for the moment, sitting on an airplane. Bill's okay, too, but I don't know if they can get out of the city." Julie's voice trembled, and she quickly changed the subject. "How are you feeling, Jon? Any strange things going on?"

"Yes, as a matter of fact. But I'm not freaking out like a lot of the folks around here. I've been feeling disoriented and out of sync. Now I'm beginning to feel bloated."

"Oh, I know. Me, too. I haven't felt this fat since I was pregnant many long years ago. At least this won't last nine months, I hope!"

"Mom, 'nothing shall be impossible unto you.' Are you sure you're not—?"

Julie laughed, almost blushing. "That would truly be a miracle at my age. Seriously, Jon, if you're not leaving the city, promise me you'll be with me psychically through this. I don't care how well connected we are on the etheric plane; there's still nothing in the world as great as a hug from you. So take very good care of yourself, okay?"

"Okay, Mom. I'll stay open for communication. Just send me a thought and we'll connect. And, Mom?"

"Yes?"

"If you've said it once, you've said it a hundred times: I know this will be an adventure like we haven't had in eons. So relax! Enjoy the roller coaster ride and don't forget how much I love you."

"You've got it," Julie said, trying to maintain lightness in her voice. "Take care, Jon. I love you."

Chapter Five

Temperatures dropped 20 degrees and the wind whistled through the trees. Julie knew it could get violent, reaching velocities of 150 to 200 miles per hour, even more on the coast. That was fierce enough to cause major damage. Tightening the hood of her jacket, she bent her head against the powerful gusts and headed down the path to the barn once again. She struggled with the heavy door, latching it behind her. She was soothed by the barn's warmth and protection, and the company of the animals felt reassuring. They had all come inside seeking shelter from the wind.

Julie secured the stall doors, fed the horses, and filled the water troughs. She scattered corn for the chickens and made sure the cats had what they needed. She wished them well on their own journeys into the unknown, and battened down the hatches, making sure everything was secure.

No doubt about it, she thought, heading back to the house, the countdown had begun. A soft lavender haze permeated the earth's aura, making everything look and feel eerily different. Julie's inner body vibrated to a sound she couldn't hear. The serenade of the outer world, usually filled with the cheerful symphony of crickets and frogs, was fading, as though coming from a great distance. An eerie silence settled across the land. The only sound was the blustery wind spiraling through the tall pines.

Temporarily refreshed, Julie descended the basement stairs. Dave had planned to turn it into a rec room for the grandkids someday, but out of necessity it had become the storage room. If things got too violent, they might have to spend some time down here. Who knew where you would be the safest? Not even the prophets had been able to fully describe what life would be like after the Photon crisis. God created the world in seven days and now He was remaking it. More than once Julie had questioned what she'd find at the end of the tunnel. A rainbow? A black hole? Only one thing was for sure: This would be a universal upheaval of the highest magnitude. Even Julie's father had been forced to admit that the unusual events happening in the world were related to something more than he could understand.

Dad. Her beloved Dad. Sitting on the basement steps, she drifted back to her first hypnotherapy session, an attempt to come to terms with the past and heal her pain. It was her first experience with past lives and she'd been very skeptical. The feelings and emotions that had been released were powerful, imagination or not.

In the mental movie, she was a young child in her crib. With her third eye, Julie saw details of her old bedroom, which were verified later. Her father, who had just come home from work, stepped into her room. He said "Hi" but he didn't touch her. Under the guidance of the therapist, Julie asked her father why he didn't give her a hug and tell her he loved her. "Men don't do that kind of thing," he told her. His parents hadn't hugged him so he hadn't known how.

Julie had cried deep, painful tears for the loss of that part of her childhood but she finally understood. He'd been a stern disciplinarian, but he had loved her.

About six months later she had the dream. It had been so incredibly real, so matter of fact, she woke Dave.

"Dad and I were talking," she explained, "and I could see him and the back of me. He was about the age he is now and smiling. All of a sudden he did this *Star Trek* thing and crystallized into a young man in his 30s. We were chatting and happy and then he put his arms around me and said, 'I love you' and I said, 'I love you, too, Daddy,' and he dissolved back into what he looks like today!"

Dave held her in his arms as she released the tears held so long in her heart.

The dream never faded. It was enough to have connected in that way. Six months later the most astounding thing happened. Julie recalled the trip back East to visit her parents. She had been standing in the kitchen, talking with her dad and told him she was tired and needed to get some rest. He agreed but he stood there, looking at her. Then he walked over, put his arms around her, and said, "I love you, sweetheart." The dream had become real.

Somehow she found her voice and whispered, "I love you, too, Dad," and made it upstairs to the privacy of her bedroom before dissolving into healing tears that lasted well into the night. The loving connection became a nightly occurrence.

On the flight home from Boston, she had written her folks a letter, telling them of her experience. Unable to send it, she filed it away as a piece of journaling for her own information.

A year later, she came across the old letter, folded and creased with time, and decided that if she were the parent of someone who had written such a message, she would want to know. With a paragraph explaining the delay, she sent it off. Talk about long days. If she had stared at the phone any harder, it would surely have disintegrated. Finally, it rang.

"We got your letter today," her father said. "I wish you had sent this before."

Julie couldn't tell where he was coming from. Her voice wavered ever so slightly. "I was afraid of what you might say, Dad. I thought you might be angry or hurt or tell me it was ridiculous."

"Well, there's no reason to think that." He sounded a little gruff. "I've sent you a letter back. You'll get it in a few days."

"I'll watch for it," she said rather inanely. It was the understatement of the year.

The letter, full of typos and crossed out words, was beautiful. He said he regretted not spending more time with her as a child and repeated all those things she had experienced under hypnosis. It was a sad commentary on the old tribal rule that "grown men don't cry." He told her that he loved her very much and he hoped she knew that.

Julie cherished the letter; she still had it. It was a giant healing step, one of understanding how the universe works on different levels. The lasting result was a very special closeness between them that had never existed before. She had finally filled that vacant hole in her soul.

As time went by, Julie stretched her father's spiritual beliefs to the limit. When she brought up reincarnation and psychic readings, he countered with "Bullshit." Her cheeks flushed hot pink and for the first time in her life, she talked back. "Do you know everything there is to know about the universe? Can you walk on water?"

When she calmed down, she said, "I respect your spiritual beliefs, Dad. All I'm asking is that you respect mine. Maybe they're not the same as yours, but what I believe is just as real to me as what you believe is to you." Then she added, her anger rising, "At least I have an open mind and I'm willing to listen and read and then accept what feels right."

"I guess I just can't say anything to you anymore," her father snapped.

"That sounds like a child talking!" she shot back and walked away, shaken to the core.

But it opened his spiritual door a crack. His curiosity had been peaked, and he'd leapt right through when he agreed to table-tip with her and Jon. Contacting spirit and loved ones who had crossed over was a new and strange experience for him.

The first session was actually kind of funny. Spirit began moving the table. Her father asked if she was doing it and looked under the table to check. It was a struggle to identify the unseen guest but they finally determined the entity to be a friend of his from childhood. Julie went through all the names she could think of, each time the table adamantly tipping "no." She'd finally pleaded with her father to concentrate and say any name that popped into his head. When she was about to abort the whole thing, he said, "Marvin Harris!"

The table literally bounced off the floor with a big "YES!" It hardly stopped tipping for joy.

After receiving the message from the spirit, her father said, "Are you sure you didn't move that thing?"

"Dad, why would I even want or need to do that? To bring in Marvin, for heaven's sake?"

"It's just so strange. I really heard that name in my head. He was my best friend for years and years. Just before he died he called and told me what I'd meant to him."

Now her father was with her mother and they watched over the family from the other side. If the predictions came true, they might all be in the same dimension soon.

Chapter Six

The cell phone jarred her out of her reverie and once again she ran up the basement stairs. "Julie, how're you doing? Are you okay?"

"Rachel!"

Rachel was a true soulmate, closer than a sister, a best friend for 30 years. She was older than Julie but she hadn't really aged since she was 39. She probably weighed 100 pounds soaking wet, but could carry a 65-pound backpack up a 14,000-foot mountain. Rachel was a true adventurer few could keep up with, least of all Julie.

"I'm fine!" Julie said. "Well, sort of, I think. Actually I'm feeling really weird and jittery. What about you?"

"Same thing. The kids and I are getting together, most of us anyway. They're spiritually aware enough to go along with me. We're at Kim's house. It's a bit crowded but we're used to that. God willing and the walls don't burst, I'll soon be seeing you in the next dimension!" Rachel laughed.

"Crowded must be the understatement of the year." Rachel had six children and a raft of grandchildren.

"Yup, you're right! But tell me, Julie, what's going on with your family? Are any of them coming? Are they okay? Is Dave there? Are you alone?" Her questions flew like bullets from a machine gun.

"I'm really doing okay. Dave is trying to escape L.A. and the earthquake. So is Bill. Kathy and the kids left Phoenix a while ago and Jean and Jerry are headed back from Tucson. Hopefully they'll arrive safely before …"

"Julie!"

"Sorry. Jon is staying in San Francisco and Chris and Ellen in Raleigh. Steve, Megan, and the boys are going camping in the Rockies."

"Camping! But you know, that might not be such a bad idea. At least they'll be close to Mother Earth and out of the city," Rachel said thoughtfully.

"That's what I was thinking. I've read that being in a natural environment might actually be the very best place to be. I'm sure they'll be guided, but the Rockies are so damn vast! It's still kind of hard to tune into them. Lots of protective veils around Steve. Lots of old pain. But that may heal soon. The good news is that I've got Max and my other four-footed friends for company. And, yes, I will see you in a few days, dear Rachel, that I know. Boy, it's good to hear your voice now, though!"

"Just wanted to check in before all the phones quit. It was hard to get through but I had to connect one more time to tell you how much I love you and what your friendship has meant to me through the years, Julie. That's all."

"We've been there for each other, dear friend. That's what it's been about for us. I know we'll both come through this with flying colors. We've done it before and we'll do it again. We'll meet on the etheric plane or wherever it is we're going. And I love you, too!"

Feeling better, Julie walked to the window. The sun was setting, casting a shimmery glow of colors on the deep lavender horizon and profiling the wind-whipped trees. Selecting some logs from the large supply piled near the stone fireplace, she coaxed the wood into a good blaze, wrapped herself up in a soft woolen throw, and curled up on the couch. Waiting was hard. Her favorite crystal was on the table and she cradled it in her hands. She could feel its vibrations and went where it led her.

Bill ran hard, gasping for air. He stopped to catch his breath and wipe the sweat from his face. Checking the big blue signs, he headed for United. If there were any chance of connecting with Dave, it would be there. At least they'd be together.

Swinging his makeshift backpack into place, he charged across the parking lot, dodging cars and people.

Julie's inner vision blurred but soon her beloved David appeared on the screen of her third eye, beads of sweat on his brow. Angry voices pierced the air.

"Why can't we leave now?"

"What's the matter with this goddamned plane! Who made this piece of crap, some garage mechanic?"

"I'll never fly on this airline again!" another yelled.

Dave could feel the heat and the rising panic in the plane as he walked up the aisle, trying to reassure passengers. The air was stagnant and heavy.

The captain's announcement was broken by static crackling throughout the aircraft. "We should be able to … gate in just a few minutes, folks," he said. "Thank you … patience. Please take your seats … leave as soon as we get the word."

A young woman with a baby in her arms suddenly jumped up and ran to the front of the plane. She was hysterical, screaming in complete terror. "Let me off! I've gotta get off! I can't breathe! I can't stand it any longer! This plane's gonna crash, I know it is! Please, you've got to open that door and let me out!"

The flight attendant began to protest that it was against the rules, but she thought better of it. The baby's crying had escalated into screeching as it reacted to its mother's fear. The flight attendant quickly opened the door and the woman fled up the jet way.

As the attendant was about to secure the hatch, she saw a man running down the jet way, three security guards close on his heels.

"Hold that door open, damn it!" he yelled. "I'm coming on board!" The security guards grabbed Bill just as he got to the plane. "Let me go, you son of a bitch! I've got to get to my kids! I know there's a seat on there and I want it!"

"Forget it, asshole!" a guard shouted. "Who the hell do you think you are? You're coming with us!"

"Dave!" Bill yelled, trying to see into the plane, "for God's sake, if you're in there, help me!"

"Oh my God!" Dave said, charging up the aisle. He reached Bill and whispered hoarsely, "Shut up, for Christ's sake! Calm down! You won't get on if you piss everyone off."

Bill took a deep breath. "Okay, okay, I'm sorry. Look, Miss, if there's a seat, I'll pay whatever it takes. There's an emergency at home and I'm really upset. I'm sorry. I lost it. You understand, don't you? Do you have kids? Please, put yourself in my shoes."

The flight attendant intervened, eager to bring peace to her plane. "Excuse me, gentlemen," she told the guards. "You were doing your job and we appreciate that. Thank you. And we do have a seat that was just vacated. If this gentleman has an emergency, he's welcome to it. We'll take care of the details later. Now, if you don't mind, I've got to close this hatch. We're about to take off."

The guards were reluctant to release Bill but with all hell breaking loose everywhere in the terminal, they ran back up the jet way. "Okay, lady! It's your funeral!" yelled the one who held Bill.

Bill was barely seated when the captain made an unofficial announcement. "We're leaving!"

Julie's crystal was downright hot. Shifting to a more comfortable position, she tuned her thoughts to Kathy and her precious cargo.

Joey seemed calm enough and Erica was sleeping again. Kathy's teeth were clenched, her chin set with determination and concentration as she hunched over the wheel. She wished Bill were there. He was always on the road when things went wrong. Her eyes drifted to the gas gauge. Nearly empty! How many miles had she gone? She wondered where they were. She had been concentrating on the road, trying to stay out of the way of other cars. The landscape was desolate, no signs, no clues. She dialed 911 on the cell phone, and then realized they were out of range.

Sensing her fear, Erica began to whimper and quickly escalated into a full-blown scream. Joey patted her head gently, not his usual mode of action. He was a rough and tumble kind of kid and tenderness wasn't his strong point. "It's okay, Erica," he whispered. "Don't cry. We'll be okay."

Sure, Kathy thought, easy for you to say. What the hell do I do now? There isn't much choice. It'll be dark in a couple of hours. Should I drive until the last drop of gas is gone? Sit on the side of the road? Cash it all in? Maybe it's the end of the road, not the side. Maybe that would be the easiest route to peace. Just let go. Who cares anyway? Her eyes stung.

Kathy's emotions had been all over the map the last few months. Julie had assured her it was happening to everyone but now she sank deeper and deeper into self-pity. It was just too much. The miles sped by, using up the fuel slowly but surely. Inevitably, the car began to sputter, losing its energy just as she was. She saw a turnout ahead, a parking area. Sweat beading her forehead, the last sputter glided her into the open space, off the pavement. "Thank you," she said leaning her head against the steering wheel.

She squeezed into the back seat, with the car seats, toys, and two kids. Kathy extracted them from their seats and backed out of the 4Runner, the gravel crunching under her feet. The rim of trees and thick bushes cast long shadows, creating an eerie scene in the middle of nowhere. In a relatively clean area under a tree, she managed to change Erica's diaper while Joey relieved himself behind a rock. Then, with her son a reluctant baby sitter, Kathy positioned herself on the side of the road, hoping to flag down a passing car. It soon became obvious that no one had any interest in picking up strangers. What with all the crime lately, she could hardly blame them. Besides, if they felt like she did, they'd be frantic to get to where they were going. Erica's cries called her back to the blanket.

Kathy settled the baby at her breast, and spoke softly to Joey who was strangely quiet. She reminded him of how they prayed at night when he went to bed, asking God to watch over them and all those he loved. She felt they should talk to God right now because they really needed His help. The power of two people gathered together magnified the strength. It didn't matter that one of them was only five years old.

With the deep intention and expectation of being heard, she prayed, "Dear God, I know you have much to do and so many people to help right now but, if You can, please help us, too. Maybe You could send an angel to give me some guidance on what to do. I know I haven't always done the right thing in this life but I've come such a long way and I'm not ready to give up, although I thought about it a while ago. I'll fight but I can't do it alone. Please, please help us now."

Her faith renewed, she made a concerted effort to focus on what she had to do this very moment. The sun had dropped behind the desert mountains and the sky had a lavender glow. The wind had gotten nasty. It would be a long cold night.

The plane taxied out towards the runway, a long line of planes in front and behind. The tower was in turmoil. Electromagnetic waves created havoc with the airwaves, and traffic controllers, frustrated and angry by the interference, had to scream into poorly functioning headsets. One controller slumped over his controls, his head in his hands. Another stormed from window to window, shouting, "I can't believe it! I just can't believe it! What the hell is going on? They're all going to get killed out there."

Pilots, already shaken by the earthquake, now felt an urgency they couldn't understand, and without guidance, didn't wait the prescribed length of time between take offs and landings. Communication with the control tower was garbled at best. Mutiny reigned on the tarmac. At least Dave's plane was moving now as silent and some not-so-silent prayers filled Flight 489. Dave and Bill mentally surrounded the plane with white light as it inched toward the runway.

Screams jarred them from their thoughts when a commuter jet landed, brakes screeching and tires smoking. It swerved out of control and missed the off ramp. It skidded off the runway, heading for their plane. Terrified passengers watched as the commuter's wing tip miraculously passed inches under the wing of the United jet.

Dave's aircraft moved ahead another hundred feet. Time seemed to stand still.

Chapter Seven

Jeannie had been sound asleep but woke with a jolt just in time to see the outline of Kathy's car as they sailed by it. "It's the car! It's the 4Runner! I know it is," she cried.

Brakes screeched and the smell of burning rubber was acrid as Jerry skidded to the side of the road, swearing softly under his breath. He backed up, not quite believing his wife but aware that she wasn't usually given to unexplained hysterics or an over-active imagination. It was dark and cold, not a good night for camping.

"Jesus, it is them!" he said.

They jumped out and ran to the 4Runner. The first thing they saw was Joey's nose pressed up against the window.

"Aunt Jeannie!" Joey shouted. "Uncle Jerry! Mom! Look! Look out the window!"

Kathy unwrapped herself from the quilt, Erica in her arms. Disbelief quickly turned to joy. "Jean! Jerry! Oh, thank you, God! Thank you!" She unlocked the doors and everyone hugged everyone, once, twice, three times.

"How did you find us?" Kathy asked.

"I'm not sure," Jean said. "Something woke me up and I saw the 4Runner. Julie would say an angel did it. What happened? What on earth are you doing here?"

"Stupid me, I was running out of gas so I just drove and drove until it was all gone. I don't even know where we are. We tried flagging down cars but no one would stop. The whole world must be running scared."

Jerry took off his coat and wrapped it around Kathy's shoulders. "Come on. Let's get you into the truck to warm up. It'll be pinched quarters but we can make it. There's room in the back for your stuff. Give me your keys and I'll get it."

In the truck, Jean tucked blankets around the threesome. She dug into her lunch bag and came up with half a sandwich, some potato chips, and an apple for them to share. There was enough food to get them to Takoma Springs.

Steve and Megan's faithful Explorer was packed to the limits. The six-year-old twins, Jesse and Michael, and their Irish setter, Rusty, took up a great deal of space and made a lot of noise. Then there were all the supplies and equipment for camping in the mountains. The constant din was getting on Steve's nerves. He felt the beginning of a migraine.

"For God's sake, Megan, can't you keep the kids a little quieter?"

"Relax, for heaven's sake. Boys will be boys, remember?"

"Sorry," Steve mumbled. He let his mind drift to his beloved mountains. The sun had set and the moon outlined the jagged edges of the peaks.

The sounds in the car began to fade like background noise at the beach. The migraine crept up the back of his neck and pounded in his temple. "Damn," he muttered. "I don't need this now."

~ ~ ~

Car lights played across the wall of Julie's living room. Someone was coming down the long driveway to the house. Gravel crunched, followed by three quick honks. Switching on the outside light, Julie went out to the deck overlooking the driveway. It was Anna and Doug, their close friends from Durango. Anna was a metaphysical playmate, a spiritual soul mate. Julie ran down the steps.

"Oh boy, it's so good to see you guys!"

"It's coming, isn't it?" Anna said, more a statement than a question. She looked pale and distraught, a mirror of what Julie was feeling inside. "I feel it, Julie. We've taken care of our animals and figured we had time to check up on you. Couldn't get through on the phone. Are you alone?"

"Not any more." Julie smiled. "Those who can make it are on their way. I wish Dave were here. But he did survive the earthquake and he's trying to get home."

Doug put his arm around her shoulders and gave her a reassuring squeeze. "He'll be okay. He has a gift of being in the right place at the right time. Trust that."

"That's true," Anna said. "And I know how you feel. I'm usually pretty calm, but I guess it's the vibrations. It's hard to prepare in advance for that."

"How about a cup of tea to settle you down?" Julie asked.

"We can't stay, Julie," Doug said. "Thanks anyway. Is there anything you need done that I can help you with? Heavy stuff? Help with the animals?"

"I think I'm as ready as I can be right now. I've gone over the list again and again. I just feel weird."

"We all do," Anna said. "I had a dream last night. A nightmare is more like it. It was a premonition and I broke out in a cold sweat and started shaking. We've been busy ever since. Have you got plenty of food and water? Is the greenhouse working?"

Julie laughed. "Anna, you and I have been making preparations for months. But your concern is much appreciated. I'll check the greenhouse again in a little while. I've harvested and dehydrated, just in case we need it. Don't worry about me. I know we'll be able to connect more closely in ways we can only imagine right now. That's the exciting part." Julie put her arms around her friends. "I hate to see you go but you two better be on your way."

"You're right. Come on, Annie. It'll take an hour to get home. The only calm people in our territory are the Native Americans. I guess they've been aware for lifetimes, haven't they?"

Albuquerque, land of flat-topped adobe houses, was so close yet so far away. The jet had been circling the airport for an hour, waiting to land. The constant turbulence and tight circling made more than a few nauseous. Bill was pale and had broken out in a clammy sweat.

Dave thought the whole trip was taking too friggin' long. Just then the intercom sounded.

"Looks like we're in line, folks," a flight attendant announced. "Make sure your seat belts are fastened and seat backs and tray tables are in their upright position. The captain says it will be a fast descent, so relax. We'll soon be on the ground."

The announcement brought a cheer from the cabin, but as the plane went into a steep bank for the turn, it felt as though they were going in upside down, and cheers turned into shrieks. Engines whined and lights blinked and the plane slowly straightened out. The nose pointed down too much in Dave's opinion, and their speed seemed to accelerate. It felt as if they were heading into a nosedive.

Suddenly Dave had an inspiration. He began singing "You Are My Sunshine." The distraction caught on and the plane was soon filled with an *a cappella* choir. It reached a crescendo just as the plane touched down. Bouncing several times, it swerved one way, then the other. Without a doubt it was the hottest landing and fastest stop Bill and Dave had ever experienced, and one they hoped to never experience again. A resounding cheer arose from the plane as it headed for the gate. Landing instructions were lost in the uproar but people stayed in their seats. They were too weak-kneed to stand up.

Bill reached across the aisle and put out his hand. "Congratulations, Dave. I knew you could sing but that has to be the damnedest performance I've ever heard." There was a touch of awe in his voice and a new respect for this stepfather of his.

"Aw, it was nothing. Don't even know why I did it. Come on. Let's get off this friggin' flying machine and find the car. We've got to make tracks fast."

Albuquerque had never looked so good.

Chapter Eight

Julie breathed deeply, enjoying the moist scent of the greenhouse, a place that always made her happy. She whistled a chorus of *You Are My Sunshine*, then frowned. Shrugging her shoulders, she checked the thermostat, blessed all things growing, and closed the door.

Back in the house, she picked up the phone to call Raleigh but there was severe interference—not quite gone but in the throes of death. She tried the computer again. It worked but she couldn't get on the Internet. No phone lines, no e-mail. She found her cell phone. Her hands shook as she dialed Chris's cell number. It rang! Her heart skipped a beat when she heard the static. A few words came through before the phone went dead. It was enough to be able to reassure Dave that his son and daughter-in-law were all right so far. Whether they were spiritually ready for the next dimension was another question.

She glanced at the clock. It had been twelve hours since she had gotten the first hit that "it" was beginning. It felt like a lifetime ago. She was tired and hungry. Julie stoked the fire against the night chill and wandered into the kitchen. She opened the fridge, closed it, and opened it again. Nothing looked good. Maybe the apple. How long would they have the refrigerator? Not much longer. Maybe she'd have that leftover turkey after all. With some crisp lettuce and mayonnaise. And a glass of cold milk. She piled the food on the counter and began making sandwiches. With everyone coming, she'd better be prepared. The line between acceptance and denial was strange, so far beyond understanding and comprehension. She wasn't going nuts; the world was.

She sat in front of the fire, eating. The sandwich was indeed tasty. The fire snapped and crackled and warmed her. Max and Sandy curled up at her feet as the wind whistled and rattled the windows. She went to the door and snapped on the light.

The treetops pointed north. A lid from a trashcan spiraled across the driveway. Max growled a warning. She should check on the animals. As she headed for her coat and boots, the power went dead.

Jerry raced through Gallup, New Mexico, heading north on Route 666, often referred to as "The Devil's Highway." Headwinds ate up the gas like crazy. In the crowded cab, Joey's little-boy babble made them laugh. Erica ate and slept.

Beams of light flashed across the desert as cars sped by in both directions. The miles ticked off, one by one.

Dave maneuvered the Bronco around stalled cars and trucks and through intersections with blinking red lights that backed up traffic. This was not the time for the faint of heart. A slow-moving black semi blocked Dave's view of oncoming traffic, causing his adrenaline to flow. Gunning the engine, he swerved to the right of the truck and onto the shoulder. He cut it too close and ripped off the side mirror. Dave grinned as they hit the open road.

Bill's face was ashen in the reflected dash lights. "Jesus, man! What're you trying to do, kill us both? I felt safer in the frigging jet, for Christ's sake!"

"Easy, Bill," he laughed. "We made it, didn't we? I didn't want to breathe truck fumes all the way home."

"I just want to be able to keep breathing, thank you very much." But Bill calmed down. He'd done crazier things himself in his younger years. "Sorry for losing it. I know you're a good driver."

"It's okay. If I was sitting over there, I'd feel the same way." No one would ever catch Dave on the passenger side, not if he could help it. Four more hours to Wind Dancer Ranch and Julie.

Steve and Megan had driven as far as they could go at night on the narrow mountain road. They felt strange and uncomfortable but attributed it to tension. The boys slept soundly in the back seat, Rusty snuggled as close as he could get to his buddies. Little boys look like angels, Megan thought, especially when they're asleep. She smiled tenderly.

Steve wanted to set up camp for the night where they were and hit the trail early in the morning. The tent would be easy to pitch. But when they stepped out of the Explorer, a gust of wind slammed them against the car with enormous force.

"Jesus!" Steve shouted. "Get back in the car. This is bad!"

They struggled with the door, made it in, and breathed a sigh of relief. "Whew! That was wild!" Megan said. "What do we do now?" It was more a statement than a question.

"I say we get comfortable right here in the car, catch some shut-eye, and head out in the morning. The boys are okay. There's no way a tent is going to stand up in this wind."

Megan crawled over the boys to get the sleeping bags. It was much cozier in the car and she could sleep anywhere. Steve worried about what was happening, concerned for his family. He wouldn't get much sleep. He certainly wouldn't have gotten any "out there."

Chapter Nine

The flashlight played over the driveway and fields as Julie struggled down the path to the barn, barely able to make headway against the howling wind. She managed to open the door and slip into the sweet-smelling building. The horses stomped their feet in greeting, their lips flapping with snorts. The goats pulled themselves up out of their cozy nests in the hay and even the cats came to get their ears scratched. Julie found the kerosene lantern and lit it. The flickering glow cast long shadows across the floor and walls. She went about the chores, shoveling, talking, and soothing her friends—and herself—as she worked.

She wasn't in any hurry to get back to the house, nor was she eager to fight the blasts of wind roaring through the valley. She sat on a bale of hay and leaned against the center post, listening to the rafters creak and grown. The hay and dust made her nose itch and after a sneeze, she settled down and opened her mind.

On her third deep breath, she realized she wasn't alone. She continued to focus on her breathing, allowing the connection with Spirit to come, not in fear but in anticipation.

"Julie."

Whether she heard it with her ears or her heart, she wasn't sure. Goosebumps raised the hair on her arms. Again, a soft male voice spoke. "Julie."

A form began to solidify in her third eye. "Dad! It's you! Boy, am I glad you're here! I've been a bit jittery being here all alone. The truth is, I'm scared."

"I know, and I've come to tell you not to fear. You're facing a challenge and part of that challenge is to extend your faith to prayers for others, both those who will be here with you and those in fear everywhere. Don't let that fear close you down or stop you from expanding the field of love beyond your own aura."

"I'll do my very best, Dad." She paused. "It will be all right, won't it?"

"It will be the way it's supposed to be. Remember the Universal Laws. You know them well, especially the Law of Attraction. What you think about will be drawn to you, whether it's fear or faith, joy or sadness. Think love for all mankind, for your world and your universe. Love and forgiveness. Forgiveness and love. Trust your intuition, dearest Julie. You must have the faith of the proverbial mustard seed. You're all in God's hands. Let the fear go."

"I'll try. I really will. Thank you for being here for me. I love you so much, Dad."

"We'll be seeing each other soon. I love you, too, Julie."

The image and voice faded into blackness and silence. She smiled. All those years of trying to get through that spiritual wall he stubbornly hid behind, and now he was preaching her script back to her.

Maybe she'd actually be seeing him soon! And Mom. And most everyone, including the great Masters of the world if she could believe what she'd been told. Gandhi, Buddha, Jesus, Kwan Yin, Mary—they'd be returning soon. Or we'll be joining them.

Whichever it was, it would occur in the Fifth Dimension. It was truly an incredible time to be on earth, Julie thought.

She could only speculate on what the predicted gifts of Spirit would be—to be telepathic, healed of all disease, and to eventually look and feel young again. It boggled her mind but rekindled the excitement she had felt and tried to share with others. This is one time the old adage, "Time will tell," would prove profound. After the Zero Point, time wouldn't matter because there wouldn't be any. For the first time ever, there would be enough of it. No one would ever run out of it.

With a deep sigh, she mentally gathered her energy back into her body, but someone knocked on the door of her subconscious again. She opened her mind to receive.

"Mom! What are you doing in the barn at this hour?"

"I thought I might sleep out here with the animals tonight, Jon."

"You who loves your toasty down comforter? Seriously, how're you doing? Everything okay?"

"I'm fine. Your grandfather just paid me a visit and put me on track again. Between his wisdom and your sense of humor, I'm doing just great. What about you?"

"I sort of listened in on some of Gramp's sermon. I can't wait to see him again. Right now, the winds are really kicking ass here but they haven't even begun to reach the peak. They could reach 200 mph, right?"

"Or more, Spirit said. I think the worst is on the fourth or fifth days of this thing, when the darkness comes."

"I know how concerned you are, Mom. We share all thoughts and emotions. No place to hide. Do you know where the others are?"

"It's hard to tell. The roads are dark and I don't 'see' any signposts. I have to trust the angels on that one."

"My energy's weakening, Mom. You're fading. Let me know when they get there."

It was all speculation. Like near-death experiences, it was a personal thing, not understood by those who'd never had one. Some would remain in the Third Dimension, continuing to deal with war and violence and fear. Others already in the Fourth Dimension and aware and open to the spiritual world would make the transition to the first level of the Fifth Dimension, a plane of love and peace.

Most psychics agreed on some of the major points, such as the time of darkness as the planet moves through the dense part of the Photon energy. During that time, people and animals would be in a heavy semi-hibernation state. The laws of physics would be suspended and no electrical or magnetic devices would work. For how long, no one knew. When the planet emerged on the other side, everything would be illuminated by a soft glow. Our psychic senses would be fully operational.

Julie called the dogs and prepared to face the violent winds whipping across the open fields. Tree limbs created strange shadows in the flashlight beam but it guided her well and she was soon safe inside. She placed a propane lamp in the big window, a beacon of light for her loved ones to follow. Then, with nothing more she could do, she retreated to the couch and her toasty blanket to wait for the dawn of a new day, a new world.

~ ~ ~

"Is this the street? Do I turn here?" Jerry asked. "It's so freaking dark, I can't see a thing! Nothing looks the same. It's spooky!"

Jean's nose was pressed against the fogged window. The blackness outside was all encompassing. The truck was buffeted by the wind, and bounced over fallen branches in the road. Her baby was restless and she was altogether uncomfortable. The headlights picked up a swinging power line just in time for Jerry to avoid it.

"Jesus Christ! It feels like we're in a goddamned hurricane. You all right back there?"

Erica began crying and Kathy soothed her. "Yeah, Jerry, we're just a bit shaken. Don't worry about us."

"For Pete's sake, Jerry, watch your language," Jean whispered. "The kids can hear you."

"Sorry, but we could have been killed, ya know."

She patted his leg and leaned forward, straining to see beyond the glow of the headlights. "We're getting close, I think."

Kathy, squeezed into the back seat with luggage and children, wasn't able to see much more than the back of Jean and Jerry's heads. She looked at Joey, whose eyes were squeezed shut, a look of deep concentration on his face.

"Now! Turn now!" Joey said.

Startled, Jerry swerved onto a road, caught a glimpse of the street sign, and said, "How the devil did he know that? Jesus! Thanks, kid. We could have spent a lot of time looking for the damn thing. Good thing you can see out."

"You shouldn't swear so much, Uncle Jerry," Joey said. "And I can't see out.

"Sure," Jerry said.

"Sometimes Joey just knows things, Jerry," Kathy said. "We think he has some telepathic abilities."

"Yeah, right." Jerry wasn't convinced.

"And Daddy's with Grandpa," Joey said. "And I think they're in Grandpa's big Bronco. They're going to meet us at Grandma's, aren't they, Mommy. Don't you believe me, Uncle Jerry?"

"Yeah, well, I sure hope you're right, Joey."

Kathy had come to respect her son's insights. They weren't always correct but right now she would grasp at any straw. "Joey, can you tell how far away your daddy is? Is he all right?"

Joey closed his eyes again. "There's a dark road and they're going awfully fast." He paused. "That's all I know."

"Thanks, honey. That was good. Will you let Mommy know if you see anything else?"

Five minutes passed in silence.

"Uncle Jerry, turn again!" Joey yelled and this time Jerry didn't question it. The kid was better than a street map, especially in the dark.

"Boy, I can't wait to stand up," Jean said. "I feel like I've gained ten pounds, and I'm so dizzy."

"Yeah. Me, too," Kathy said. She wasn't sure she could even stand up. "At least we're almost there. It feels like a lifetime since we left Phoenix. And I could sure use a bathroom."

"Me first!" Jeannie laughed.

"No, me!" Joey giggled.

"Hey, you guys, I'm driving. I get it first, okay?"

They were quite light hearted by the time they saw the light in the window.

"There it is, Mommy! There's Grandma's house!" Joey shouted.

They pulled up to the big house in the meadow, the truck rocking in the wind, and all bowed their heads in a prayer of thanks.

Julie sat bolt upright. What was that? She'd heard something. Disoriented, she untangled herself from the blanket and tripped over Max, who yelped and growled. Julie looked out the big window and shouted with joy. "They're here! Someone's here!" She raced to the door, dogs barking at her heels.

Never was anyone happier to see their loved ones than the windblown troops from the south and Julie Armstrong. After hugs and trips to the bathroom, Jerry struggled with luggage and Joey and Erica snuggled up in their grandmother's arms.

"Grandma, it was hard. We had to stay in the car so-o-o long! Can I play with Max and Sandy?"

"Watch out for the candles, Joey. There aren't any lights so watch where you're going," Kathy warned.

"Come on," Julie said, "I'll get you something to eat and you can tell me all about the trip. Thank God you found each other. I want all the details!"

They gathered around the old dining room table, candles casting a soft glow. The plate of sandwiches quickly disappeared. Everyone shared their adventure as they compared the strange physical changes they were experiencing. Erica nursed and Joey snuggled in his Grandma's arms, basking in the deep spiritual love connection they shared. Max and Sandy curled up for a well-deserved snooze.

"What's gonna happen, Grandma? Are we going to die?"

"No, Joey. We're going to be just fine. Some strange things are going on in our world and it makes us feel uncomfortable," Julie explained. "But you and I know that God watches over us and sends his angels to help us when we need help—sometimes even when we don't. Your special angels are with you right now, making sure you're okay, ready to protect you from harm. All you have to do is trust and know you'll be absolutely safe, no matter what. Can you do that?"

"Is that all I have to do, Grandma?"

"Yes, honey, that's all."

"Oh, boy! I can do that. My angel comes to play with me lots of times. He's neat and fun and makes me laugh. I'd like to have him baby-sit me and Erica but Mom says she needs someone she can see."

"I'm afraid I'd have to agree with your mom. Does your angel have a name?"

"Yup. I call him Mister G but he said I could call him whatever I want, he didn't mind. But I like Mister G so that's what I call him. He tells me things sometimes and sometimes I just know things."

"Yeah, you do, Joey," Jerry said. "I don't know how you knew when to turn but you did. Smart kid you've got there, Kathy."

"Thanks. Sometimes it's a bit unnerving, having a five-year-old read your mind."

"Speaking of that," Julie said, "I know I've said this before but after this Shift happens, we'll all be able to read each other's minds. Trouble is, we might not know whose mind we've tapped into. Sounds real confusing to me but I expect it might be something like Jon and I do now. It might be a good thing, especially if there's no other communication available."

"It's just too much to comprehend," Jean said, shaking her head. "I know what you and Jon do, and sometimes I've even experienced knowing things before they've happened. But much of what I've read is so far out, so unbelievable. Sometimes it's easier not to think about it. Then this Photon thing comes along and I wish now I'd paid more attention."

"Yeah, me, too," Kathy said.

"Well, it's never too late, guys," Julie laughed. "But right now let's do a quick tour of the house so you'll know where stuff is and what we'll be able to do, depending on what happens. Let's face it, it's really a crap shoot for me, too, at this point."

A gust of wind rattled the front windows, making the candles flicker. Joey stepped closer to his grandmother and slipped his hand into hers.

Chapter Ten

Chris got the phone call in the middle of the night. "Armstrong, we need you on duty ASAP. Get your gun and get down here. We've got problems."

Raleigh was in a complete blackout, and rioting was in full swing. People were in a panic and wanted to know what was happening. All the usual links to the outside world had been cut off. There was no power, no heat, no air conditioning, no refrigeration, no nothing. Chris could only imagine what was happening in the other big cities.

"Please don't go, Chris," cried Ellen. "I'm frightened. I feel awful, like my whole body is shaking. Maybe it's the flu. Or it could have something to do with my—Chris, there's something I need to talk to you about, something important. You might get hurt out there. I need you, too!"

"Ellie, I've got to go. I don't know what's going on but I won't be long. You'll be okay."

Chris was puzzled by his wife's reaction. She was usually pretty calm and level-headed. She had to be to face the crap she'd dealt with in courtrooms. "Look, honey, I don't think it's the flu. I think—and I hope I'm wrong—that Julie might have been right."

"We agreed Julie had gone over the edge on this one. Are you saying it really is that dimensional thing? Is that what's happening, Chris? Tell me, is that what you think it is?"

"It fits. It all fits. That's why I got all those supplies and candles and stuff. It made Julie and Dad happy at the time. Ellen," Chris said, putting his arms around her, "don't leave the apartment. Keep the doors locked and the windows closed."

She clung to him and he could feel her shaking. He debated whether to leave, to defy his orders. But the urge was strong, almost actual words, telling him to hurry. "Look, you rest and I'll get back as soon as I can. I've got to go, honey." Gently kissing the lips of the woman he loved with all his heart, he pulled away from her grasp. "I love you, El." The door closed behind him.

The streets were a mess. Out-of-control gangs roamed everywhere, breaking windows and starting fires. It was reminiscent of the Los Angeles riot back in the days of Rodney King, back before the city was cleansed to the point of damn near disappearing. What in the name of God could he do here? He hated carrying a gun. He had never had to use it and he certainly didn't want to start now. That's why he'd gotten into investigations, to get away from physical violence. He felt as though he was stepping into a time warp or a third World War.

He rounded a corner just in time to see two women running down the middle of the street in the glare of his headlights. "What the hell—"

Chris' brakes screeched. He turned on his blue and red flashing lights and jumped out of the car. The women were screaming and a gang of angry-looking guys was in hot pursuit. Flinging the back door open, he grabbed the younger one as she came close and shoved her in, shouting, "Get on the floor!" The other one followed. He turned toward the gang. Gun pulled, stance set, he watched them begin to slow down.

"That's it right there! Don't come any closer or I'll shoot!" Chris yelled.

They blasted a barrage of angry threats at him.

"We want the chick!"

"I wanna fuck the black bitch! Let me at her!"

"I'll take the old hag!" another voice jeered.

His heart pounding, Chris yelled, "Get outta here or I'll turn you all in! Back off! Go back to the holes you slimy bastards crawled out of! Get the hell outta here before I let ya have it!"

The gang seemed to hit a wall and did not go any further. They milled around, looking for another victim, looking for more trouble.

"Fuck, man! Take 'em!" the leader yelled. "There's plenty more where they came from!" They turned into the darkness and disappeared in the night.

Shaking, Chris got back in his car, his knees weak. "Hey, it's okay," he said gently, looking over the back seat. "They've gone. You can come up now." The younger woman, a teenager, was sobbing and the older woman was still terrified. "You okay?" Chris asked.

"Oh, mister, you're an answer to our prayers," the mother said, recovering her composure and holding her daughter tightly in her arms. "Thank you, Lord, thank you! Angels come in all shapes and sizes and you must be ours. I don't know how to thank you."

"Where do you live? Where can I take you?" Chris asked.

"It's gone. They burned it down. We don't have a place to go. We'll just get out. Maybe we can find some friends."

"No, I can't let you do that. If it's not these guys, there'll be others. I don't know what's going on but it's not safe for anyone out there tonight. I'm taking you home with me. You can stay there for a while until things settle down." If they ever do, he thought to himself. Ellen would be surprised but what else could he do? He wasn't going to feed them to the slaughterhouse; there was enough killing going on. At least he could save these two.

Spinning the car around, he gunned the motor and headed home.

Dave's headlights picked up the eerie swaying of the tall pines and aspens as the Bronco raced along the country roads of rural Southern Colorado. Home was closer with each passing mile. Dave's knuckles were white as he gripped the wheel.

He desperately wanted to reach home before the fuel quit working or the damn cars died on the road. A hell of a wind was kicking up and he didn't like it. Muscles taut and eyes glued to the road, he picked up speed on the straight stretches. But as they rounded a bend on Highway 84, he slammed on the brakes. The Bronco skidded to a screeching halt and the smell of burning rubber stung their nostrils.

"Jesus Christ," Bill said. "What's that?" He leaned forward, straining to see out the windshield.

The wind was even worse than they'd realized. A tree two feet in diameter lay across the road.

"Shit!" Dave slouched down into the seat. The sides of the road were impassable, with a deep ditch on one side and an impossibly steep bank on the other. There were no other roads nearby. "Any ideas?" he asked.

"No, but we've got to get around it somehow."

"I know, damn it, but how?"

"We could jack it up maybe, move it a few inches ..."

"Oh, come on, be reasonable! That tree weighs more than a ton. Dave's brow was covered with cold clammy sweat. He turned his face to the night sky. "Please, God, help us. We need a miracle!"

Bill echoed his words. They looked at each other, helpless and frightened.

All of a sudden, Dave let out a hoop. "I've got it!" he shouted. "Get some rocks, dead wood—anything you can find! We're going to build a ramp, by God! Two, actually. One for each wheel! We're gonna do some jumping!"

The rocks and heavy debris began to grow as they fitted them together as tightly as possible. Bill measured the wheel span and adjusted one of the growing ramps toward the middle. Hands bleeding and clothing torn, they finally completed their engineering feat and ran back to the Bronco. Dave backed it up for a running start.

"Gun the bastard!" Bill yelled, his adrenaline flowing. "Come on, baby! Take us for the ride of our lives!"

The engine roared as Dave pressed the gas pedal to the floor. They hit the ramp at 80 miles an hour and flew over the tree and through the air as though in slow motion. It was one hellova ride. They both let out war hoops when they landed with a thud. The Bronco bounced several times but stayed on the road.

"We did it! We flew!" Bill shouted. "Christ, did you see how far we went? How far do you think we sailed? Man, we caught some air!" he said as they gave each other the high-five.

Dave took a deep breath and a little grin tweaked the corners of his mouth. "It wasn't too bad, was it? Good truck, good wheels, lots of power. Better than a hole in one. I think we got some help from the Guy upstairs."

"Yeah! That was a great lift! Man, I'll never forget that! How can you be so bloody calm?"

"I trust my wheels. Or it's age." He shot a half smile at Bill.

Their wildly pumping adrenaline began to slow down, but not the Bronco. Ninety miles an hour on narrow country roads took concentration. They were within an hour of home, barring any more unforeseen deterrents.

Dave began to think about Julie and the rest of their family. He wondered who was where, if they were safe, scared, in trust. He felt like he'd been out of touch with his wife forever.

Joey sat on Julie's lap, eyes closed. Candlelight flickered across his face, giving him a ghostly appearance.

"Wow! That's like watching TV!" he exclaimed, jumping to the floor.

"What, honey? What are you talking about?" Julie asked.

"The truck! I just saw a truck like Grandpa's flying through the air. It was like it came off a ski jump." His eyes were wide with excitement.

"Joey doesn't need TV," Jean laughed. "He's got a great imagination."

"Maybe so, maybe not," Julie said thoughtfully. "Joey, did you see anyone in the car?"

"Yeah, I think there were two guys."

"Did the truck land safely after it went flying?" Julie's heart pounded.

"I don't know. It was so great! It flew like an airplane!"

There weren't any ski jumps between here and Albuquerque that Julie knew of. No hills that would qualify for an air flight. But it had to be Bill and Dave. Where were they? What had happened?

"Joey, would you keep my chair warm for a minute, honey? I'll be right back." Julie headed for the living room. Kathy handed the baby to Jean and followed her.

"What's up, Julie? Do you think it was them?"

"I'm sure of it. But I want to see if I can tune in. I think I'd have known if something had gone really wrong."

"The energy of two is stronger than one," Kathy said. "Let's do it together."

"Good idea."

They sat cross-legged, facing each other, holding hands. The wind howled as Julie whispered a prayer of protection and opened her mind to receive. At first she sensed the wind bending and breaking trees. Then the familiar Bronco enveloped her, the smell and feel of the leather seats, the sound of the big all-weather tires humming on pavement. Slowly the vision of her husband began to form in her mind. He was with Bill, both tense and alert, the Bronco racing hell bent for leather.

Dave cocked his head to one side. "Have you ever raced a horse, balls out, full speed ahead?" he asked.

"What the hell are you talking about?"

"I don't know. I just got this thought about Orion, my horse, and racing and leather and .... Don't mind me. I don't know what I'm thinking or doing half the time anymore."

"Hang in there, Dave. You'll be okay."

~ ~ ~

"They're all right," Julie smiled. She squeezed Kathy's hands and saw a tear run down her cheek. "He's safe, honey. It won't be long."

"It's not that so much, Julie. We've just had a real hard time lately. The kids are really demanding and there never seems to be enough money and he travels so much. It just makes it hard. I want the kids to have a real family, Julie, but there are times I've wondered if Bill and I should even stay together. We've worked hard on it. We've been to some counselors. We've tried to communicate but it hasn't been working. I know he's stressed and I try to give him his space but I'm tired, too. When I realized what was happening, you know, the Shift and your phone call, my heart almost cracked open. All I wanted was for Bill to be with us, to be able to tell him how much I loved him." Tears rolled down her cheeks. "I was so scared, Julie! I was afraid I wouldn't see him again!"

Julie held Kathy close. She knew that feeling of deep love, too. Sometimes it took a frightening event to pull it out of the depths of mundane everyday life in order to get in touch with the raw emotion once again.

"Mommy, mommy!" Joey ran across the room and threw his arms around his mother's neck. He leaned his head back and studied her face. "You're crying!" he said.

"It's okay, Joey. I'm just glad Daddy's almost here." She gave him a reassuring hug. "And yes, I've been a little upset but everything is going to be just fine. I can feel it, can't you?"

"Yup, it is. I know it. Oh boy! I can't wait!" he said, jumping up and down.

They checked the lantern in the window and felt the house shudder with another violent gust of wind.

Chapter Eleven

The Bronco lights played across the fields and trees of Takoma Springs. Except for an occasional car, the town was dark and desolate. A few lanterns or candles flickered through windows but most were dark.

Then through the trees Dave caught a glimpse of the light in his window, his Wind Dancer Ranch. His heart skipped a beat as he turned into the long driveway. Bill was out of the car before it stopped.

Julie stood back and waited until Dave took her in his arms. He held her close, as though he'd never let her go again. "Are you okay, babe?" he asked, looking deeply into her eyes.

"I am now, sweetheart. I knew you were coming. I knew in my heart you'd get here, but it's so good to see you in person." Julie returned the hug with a smile.

"I've got a lot to tell you but now isn't the time. What do I need to do?"

"Everything's under control, I think. Just help me keep everyone from panicking when things start happening. They're doing really well. They seem to have gotten the message that what you believe is what you'll get. But we need to keep everyone on track, including me."

"Where do we stand, time-wise?"

"I think we're heading into the third day."

"Dearest Julie, do you know how much I love you?"

"About as much as I love you, darling."

"I love you more."

The Explorer rocked with each fierce gust of wind. Steve's heart pounded as adrenaline flipped his fight-or-flight mechanism into high gear. His eyes ached from trying to see in the darkness. As the sky lightened, he realized that they'd actually driven a good distance into the woods but the four-wheel drive could take them no farther. Reluctantly he had to acknowledge what was happening.

He and Megan had been through some terrifying disasters with earthquakes and storms. More than once he'd thought they weren't going to make it. But he hadn't been able to take that final leap of faith into the Photon thing. It was too much, just too much. Stuck now with his precious family, his reason for living, he couldn't just sit and do nothing.

"Megan! Wake up! Wake up, Megan," he whispered urgently. Then louder, "Megan!"

"Mmmm, go away," she mumbled, pulling the sleeping bag over her head.

"No! Megan, we have to leave the car. We've got to find a safe place to be and we haven't got much time!"

Her eyes grew big as she came up out of a deep sleep. "What is it, Steve? What's happening? Where are we?"

"We made it to the trail head last night but we've got to get out of here. We've got to find some kind of shelter. It's too late to go back home."

"Why? Why is it too late? Boy, is that wind howling! My stomach hurts. It feels like I swallowed a basketball."

"That's part of it, Megan. It's the Shift. It's here. It's happening and we've got to find a safe place to see it through or we might not make it." Steve began to sweat.

"What are you talking about? What Shift?"

"I didn't want to scare you but it's what Mom's been talking about and we're in trouble!"

"Okay, okay. Take it easy. I want to know what you felt you couldn't share, Steve, but not right now." Her voice was tight. "You were here on a survival trip once, right?"

"Yeah, I was. I remember a cave. It would be protected, I think. If I can find it again—and if it isn't already being used by an animal that doesn't want company." He dismissed that possibility and leaned over the back of the seat to jostle his sons. "Come on, guys, time to rise and shine. Got a lot of hiking to do today."

"But, Daddy," Mike whined, "I just went to sleep."

"I know, tiger, but we have to move now. The wind will make it slow going so we need some extra time. Come on, Jesse. Time to get up."

The boys were too young to understand the drama unfolding in their lives. They loved the mountains and had camped out often but something unusual was making everyone very tense. They pulled themselves out of their sleeping bags and announced the need to pee. Steve helped them out of the Explorer and instructed them to shoot with the wind, not into it.

Megan tugged on her husband's sleeve. "What's happening, Steve? You're scaring me. The boys are so little. What if ..."

"Shhh. We'll make a game of it, Megan. It'll be okay." He paused, and added quickly, "It has to be."

She didn't quite believe him, although she wanted to. Preparing the backpacks, she found some power bars for their breakfast, put the small packs on the boys, donned her own, and stood ready for action. Heads down, they stayed close together, glad for warm clothing and the strength to push forward as they began the trek into the wilderness.

PART TWO

The Darkness

The LORD is my shepherd; I shall not want. He maketh me to lie down in green pastures; he leadeth me beside the still waters. He restoreth my soul: he leadeth me in the paths of righteousness for His name's sake.

Ye though I walk through the valley of the shadow of death, I will fear no evil: for thou art with me; thy rod and thy staff they comfort me.

Thou preparest a table before me in the presence of mine enemies: thou anointest my head with oil; my cup runneth over.

Surely goodness and mercy shall follow me all the days of my life: and I will dwell in the house of the LORD for ever.

The 23rd Psalm

Chapter Twelve

Chris burst into the apartment. Ellen pulled herself out of bed and stumbled to the living room to find two black women standing behind her husband. She stopped short, her mouth open. The older, plump woman's arm was around the shoulders of a slender young girl whose hair was braided with colorful beads. Her eyes studied the floor in front of her.

"Ellen, I'd like you to meet …" Chris turned to them. "I'm sorry, I don't know your names."

The older woman stepped forward. "My name is Mary and this is my daughter, Emma. We're sorry to intrude. You see, this wonderful man here saved us from being killed and insisted on bringing us here. We can go now. We'll be all right."

"Oh no, no! I'm glad he could help you," Ellen said, regaining her composure. "Please, sit down. I'll get you something to drink." She glanced at Chris, who gave her a look of gratitude. He followed her into the kitchen.

"I'm so glad you're home, Chris. What's happening out there?"

"The city's gone crazy. People are running scared, not caring a damn about anything, acting like wild animals. It's out of control. No electricity, no communication." He locked the outside door and removed his holster, laying it carefully on the table within reach.

As Ellen set a cup of coffee in front of Mary, her hand shook. "Don't be frightened, ma'am," Mary said. "There's a lot happening but God is watching over us. If we just believe that He's taking care of us, we'll be just fine."

"You better believe I was scared back there," Emma said. "I thought we were done for. But Mama says we're meant to do bigger things, and we're gonna get through the Shift." She hung her head and mumbled, "I hope we can stay here 'til it's over."

"Jesus," Chris said, the color draining from his face. "That's what's really happening, isn't it?" He glanced at Ellen, then turned to the visitors. "Of course you can stay here."

"We're in for a rough ride but it's nothin' to be afraid of," Mary said. "That's why the folks in town are outta control. In just a few days, there'll be peace. It's God's plan." She glanced around the kitchen. "Have you got some water and candles and a first aid kit here?"

"Yes, we have some things," Ellen said. "But I don't know if we've got enough. Oh dear, what do I need to do?"

"Trust," Mary said matter-of-factly.

"Then," Emma said with a reassuring smile, "comb that pretty brown hair of yours and put on some clothes. You'll feel better."

"You're right. If you'd like to wash up, there's a bathroom right down the hall. First door on the left. Here's a candle. I'll be back in a minute."

Chris followed Ellen to their bedroom. "Was it okay, Ellie, bringing them back here? I couldn't leave them in the middle of nowhere with all that's happening. They can sleep in the living room. I'll go get some more food if you want."

Ellen glared at him. "Don't you dare leave this condo! It is *not* an option. We've got enough food and water." Her tone softened. "They seem very nice. What happened to them out there?"

"A gang was chasing them. The bastards were going to rape them, then who knows? I've never seen anything like it. I stopped them with the gun but I couldn't shoot it. It's just not in me, Ellen. I want to keep peace but not by shooting people."

"I'm so proud of you, honey. You're a gentle soul and I love you for it."

A sudden gust of wind rocked the building.

I'm thirsty, Mom," Mike shouted into the wind. "And I'm tired. When are we gonna stop?"

"Yeah, me too, Mom," Jesse said. "And I need to pee. Now."

"Okay, kids, I hear you. Steve, we've really got to take a break!" Megan shouted. "Can we find a sheltered spot somewhere?"

Steve hated to stop for even a minute. It wasn't fear as much as an intensely anxious feeling. Something in his gut urged him forward. But Megan was right.

"There's a gully that way!" he yelled, pointing west. "Let's see if we can get out of the wind over there!"

The dried up wash was fairly deep and afforded a small measure of protection. They unstrapped their packs and relieved their aching bladders. A quick snack seasoned with blowing sand helped, and they suited up again for the trek. The sun was coming up.

~ ~ ~

"Julie, can I talk to you a minute? Alone?" Jean looked pale.

"What is it, honey? Are you okay?" Julie led her into the living room, the candle flickering as they moved.

"I don't know. I think so. I've got this funny feeling. My stomach feels so tight and hard. I'm worried about my baby, Julie."

"The baby isn't due for a few more weeks, is it?"

"Not according to the doctor's calculations. But with the long ride and the excitement and everything, maybe something's happening early. Oh, Julie, do you think it might be coming?" Her voice trembled and her eyes grew wide.

"I doubt it, Jeannie. If it's a contraction, it's probably just false labor. You'll get lots of those before the actual labor starts. Your body's preparing all the time so it'll be easier when the birth really begins."

"I've been getting them for a few weeks already. I didn't want to worry Jerry about it. But you're right; it's probably nothing. I've just never done this before and I don't know what to expect. We've practiced the breathing stuff but I'm not at all sure I want to go through it without drugs."

"You'll be fine, Jeannie. Talk to Kathy. She's gone through two natural births. On the second one, we used hypnosis and that helped a lot. I won't tell you it doesn't hurt; it does. But it's a good kind of hurt. You'll be bringing your child into the world, a new beginning, a new life. That's an incredible accomplishment. It's one of those wonderful things that we as women get to experience. I've always felt a little sorry for the dads. They don't get to feel that deep, intense bonding that comes from carrying a baby and giving birth. Then again, if they did, there'd probably be zero population growth," she laughed. "Be happy, Jeannie.

We're all here for you. Everything will be just fine." Julie hoped she sounded more confident than she felt.

"There it is! There's the cave!" Steve shouted, pointing half way up the side of the cliffs.

"Where?" Megan asked, looking up. "Oh, I see it. How can we get there?"

"We'll find a way. I did it before; I can do it again. We have to go slow and be careful. I'll take the boys up one at a time, then come for you. I don't know about Rusty. Come on, let's go!"

The rock wall was steep and unforgiving and they hadn't thought to bring climbing gear. Megan's heart pounded with fear for her children but she couldn't let it show.

"What if there's an animal in there?" Jesse asked.

"Then he'll eat you up," Mike said.

"Mommy, I'm scared!" Jesse wailed.

"Michael, for Pete's sake, zip your lip! Daddy will check it all out before we get there. And besides, what kind of an animal would want to climb in and out of a place like that every day!"

"How's Rusty gonna get up there?" Jesse asked.

"Let's cross one bridge at a time, Jesse. Don't worry. Daddy will figure it out."

Steve advanced up the cliff, searching for foot and handholds, testing each step and committing them to memory as he climbed, the wind whipping at his clothing and pack. Thirty feet had never looked so high as he inched his way up. Several times he had to backtrack from a dead end. Sheer survival left no other choice. They had to get into the cave.

Rocks jarred loose and tumbled down the cliff and the wind sent dust swirling around him, stinging his eyes. Sweat poured down the inside of his shirt. He didn't dare look down.

Then he was there. He pulled himself up over the lip and tried to stand up. His knees shook and a gust of wind shoved him against the side of the opening. Struggling for balance, he turned on the flashlight and carefully stepped into the dark cavern.

Swinging the beam around, he checked the shadows carefully. The cave was about 12 feet deep and angled so that it was protected from the wind. They'd be okay as long as the wind direction didn't shift. Animals had used it, no doubt about that. Something scuttled past him and ran out of the cave. He dropped his pack, took a deep breath, and headed back down to the canyon floor.

Megan bit her lip. Heights scared her. All she wanted to do at this point was strip off the tight pants and breath deeply. She had never been this bloated, even with PMS. She looked at the boys and saw that they looked puffy, too

"You guys feel all right?"

"Sorta," Mike said.

"Kinda," Jesse answered.

Megan gave them a reassuring smile.

Steve jumped the last few feet and felt a rush of relief. Rusty offered a welcome bark.

"Steve, what are we going to do about Rusty? He can't climb those rocks. When you take the boys up there, he'll go bonkers."

"Yeah, you're right. Don't worry. I'll figure something out. Okay, guys, which one goes first?"

"Me, me!" Mike yelled, jumping up and down.

"Okay, then let's get you aboard. Megan, I need him tied tightly to my back with these straps. I'll be carrying you up like a backpack, Mikey. Don't wiggle or squirm around. Don't yell or grab my hair or anything like that. Got it?"

"Yeah. I'll be good, Daddy."

"I know you will, fella. Just relax and enjoy the adventure, all right?"

Megan worked the straps around and under. She secured them and double-checked her work. It took all her strength to smile. "You look like a poppa monkey carrying his baby off into the jungle. Anyone want a banana?" There were no takers. "Tally ho and good luck, guys. Be careful!"

"Bye, Dad and Mikey. See you soon!" Jesse shouted.

Megan cuddled Jesse in her lap and offered a silent prayer. She was beyond the asking stage and demanded they be kept safe.

The wind-whipped dirt and sand stung their faces as Steve carefully made his way up the cliff with his precious cargo.

"Are we almost there, Dad?"

"Almost, tiger. Just a few steps more."

The minutes ticked by. With a final burst of energy, his boot in the last foothold, Steve boosted himself over the edge. He settled Mike against the protected wall with instructions not to move an inch, then left.

He reached the canyon floor once again and they tied Jesse on like a papoose. Jesse pulled his head down into his jacket and held onto Steve's neck. He didn't move a muscle. Jesse wanted to cry with relief when they reached the safety of the cave but he didn't want Mike to see tears. He'd never live it down.

Steve slumped to the floor, exhausted and thirsty. The boys pestered him about how he planned to get Rusty up the cliff and it annoyed him that he didn't have a clue. Tying the dog on his back didn't seem to be an option.

"How about putting him in your backpack?" Jesse offered.

"Are you kidding? He's seventy pounds of squirming fur, muscle, and bone. Neither of us would make it!" The boys' sad eyes broke his heart. "Okay, okay. I'll give it a try. What the heck. How about saying some prayers, starting now."

"You bet, Dad. We'll say all the prayers we know," Jesse said.

They emptied the bag, strewing the contents on the dirt floor. The boys sat cross-legged, fingers interlaced. Steve smiled when he heard Mike say, "Now I lay me down to sleep …"

Once again he descended the rocks, this time with an empty backpack and a pocket full of dog biscuits.

Rusty seemed to have ten legs and was as stable as a mound of gelatin but, after much struggling, Steve and Megan finally maneuvered him into the pack. Megan wavered between concern for the safety of her husband and laughter at the absurdity of the scene before her. Rusty's paws rested on Steve's shoulders, his head higher than Steve's, slobbering drool on Steve's head. Rusty's bottom half was cramped into the pack and he barked his indignity.

Steve muttered something profane under his breath but relaxed a little when he heard Megan's stifled giggles. He helped her put on her pack and sent her on her way with a pat on her rear. It felt as though he'd been rock climbing for days instead of hours. His body ached and burned. He glanced at his watch. It had stopped.

Rusty's persistant barks echoed in Steve's ears. The treats helped. The wind howled and Steve felt weird inside and out. His body hurt and his head vibrated. He silently asked his Guardian Angel to accompany him.

Steve was relieved when he saw that Megan had made it up safely. Ten more feet and he'd be there.

Without warning just a few feet from the ridge, Rusty leaped onto Steve's shoulders and jumped onto the ledge. The jolt knocked Steve off balance. He lost his grip and started falling backwards.

"Oh, God! Help me!" he screamed, clawing the air.

"Steven!" Megan screamed in horror, watching Steve grab at nothing.

Later, Megan tried to describe to Steve what she'd witnessed. "The plastic straps that were holding Rusty in must have slipped off. They just weren't there any more and you were falling, and then it was like you hit an invisible trampoline. Suddenly you were back against the cliff, hanging on, and I don't *know* how you got there. You could have died, Steve!" Tears of relief rolled down her cheeks as she clung to him.

"Yeah, Dad, it was cool. You're some climber," Mike said. Jesse simply held Steve's hand and stared in awe, wondering how he had done it.

"I don't know," Steve said, visibly shaken. "I yelled. I was sure it was all over, and then something seemed to give me a push. Maybe it was the wind. Maybe a gust hit me just at the right time and … Megan, do you believe in angels?"

"I do now. I just saw one."

Chapter Thirteen

Dave, Jerry and Bill struggled to nail the large sheets of plywood over the windows before they blew out. Gale-force winds whipped the boards around, making them difficult to handle. It was a hurricane without the rain and Dave cursed himself for insisting on large picture windows. If the wind didn't break them, the errant plywood might.

He had accused Julie of living in fear of a future no one could predict but she had called it being "realistic." He owed her one. There was a fine line between being prepared for the worst and believing there wasn't a need for it. A fight between Third-Dimensional thinking and Fifth. "It will be given unto you according to your beliefs." That was the bottom line, he thought, driving in a nail. We're about to see just how strong our beliefs really are. One by one the boards were hammered into place.

For someone who was so well-prepared for this thing, his wife was sure antsy this morning. She wouldn't tell him what was going on, just that there wasn't any need to worry about things that might not happen. He knew his Julie, though. Something was definitely cooking.

A gust of wind shook the house in Takoma Springs with a force that pinned the men to the wall. The last sheet of plywood had been nailed over the large picture windows just in time. They inched their way to the door and waited for the gale-force wind to let up before letting themselves in. Flickering candles cast shadows in the darkness and the house creaked and groaned.

"Man! Where did that blast come from!" Jerry said in awe of the raw power outside.

"It was like getting caught in a crushing wave," Bill said. "It happened so damn fast! Pow! And that was it. I couldn't move!"

Dave frowned. "I hope the barn stays in place and the animals are okay. There's no way I can get out there to check on them now."

"This is scary," Jerry said, pacing in circles, his eyes large with fear.

"Lighten up, Jerry. Try not to think of it as scary. There's an incredible change taking place in the universe right now. Focus on trust and love and you won't be frightened."

"Yeah. Jeannie's been preaching this stuff at me but to be honest, I couldn't buy it. Maybe I should've paid more attention. I'll work on it."

"No, don't *work* on it, just *do* it. You can do and be anything you want just by thinking about it. That's the beauty of knowing. There's no work involved." Julie would have been proud of him, Dave thought.

"He's right, Jerry," Bill said. "I've been through a lot of shit in my day and I sometimes still forget. If it weren't for trust and love, I'd be dead by now."

"Daddy! Daddy!" Joey, dragging his well-worn teddy bear by one arm, wrapped himself around Bill's leg. "Something hit the house and it made a lot of noise and I'm scared!"

Bill picked up his son and whirled him in a circle. "It's okay, Joey. A big gust of wind aimed for our house to make sure we were all awake and paying attention. We want to be able to remember everything about this wonderful adventure so we can tell Erica about it when she grows up. And your cousins, Mike and Jesse. Even the baby that Aunt Jeannie will be having. Can you think of anything else you want to tell them about this exciting time?"

Joey mulled it over. "I think I'll tell them how I helped Uncle Jerry get here. And how you covered the windows and the room is dark and we have candles." He paused, then added, "I know! I'll tell them about Mister G!"

"Who's Mister G?" Jerry asked.

"He's my friend who tells me things. Like, not to be afraid—like he just did when I woke up. And he plays with me, too."

"Is he here now, in the house?" Jerry asked.

"Yes, silly! But you can't see him. Only I can see him! He's *my* friend!"

"Okay. Sure. I get it." Jerry gave Bill a look that said, "Sorry about your kid." He shrugged. "What the heck. There's enough strange stuff going on so why not invisible people, too? I think I'll go find Jeannie."

Dave shook his head. "Jerry's got a lot to learn in the next few days." "Help him if you can, Bill. We want him to make the transition with us."

He wished the rest of the kids were with them. God only knows what they're experiencing. He hoped they weren't frightened. Dave went looking for Julie and found her in a deep trance in her meditation room. He quietly retreated to the kitchen for his comfort food, popcorn and a cold beer.

Jon awoke to the scream of sirens, but the short nap had replenished his system. He'd learned the art of simply saying "sleep" and awakening refreshed four hours later. Sleep had fascinated him ever since he had stumbled onto lucid dreaming research at Stanford University. Manipulating his dreams was a major step forward, not to mention roaming the universe by simply directing himself in the dream state.

Rolling over, he pulled the pillow over his head and reflected on the bizarre changes over the last two years, the "quickening" as it was called.

He'd tried to share his insights and knowledge with others. Friends laughed at his explanations. "Look at it this way," he told Stan, a good friend. "The earth used to resonate at seven point eight hertz and so did we. Then it began creeping up, and you and I and all living things had to adjust. Remember when a whole month passed by and we couldn't remember what we'd done? Scientists found the earth was vibrating at twelve hertz and escalating, but it was hushed up. Even they were afraid. Now it's really getting wild. I'm not sure where it'll end but the peak will be the Zero Point."

"Man, you're out of your frigging mind!"

"Hey, guy, it's happening," Jon persisted. "You've gotta at least consider it. There's gonna be a lot of shit going on but if you're aware of it, you won't get scared. It's for your own good, buddy."

It was like trying to open a locked steel door with a toothpick. Stan and a few other friends found things to do that didn't include Jon. It had been a lesson for him, this detachment thing. Detach first from things. It was okay to have and enjoy "things" but, if they all disappeared, that would be okay, too. Understanding and accomplishing it had been difficult. It didn't mean not loving or caring for others; it just meant calling back the energy cords connecting you. This released and empowered people so they would be responsible for their own outcomes.

Stan would make his own choices. That's just the way it was.

Sirens pierced through his pillow and wind whistled around the eaves. Jon whispered, "Peace, be still," visualizing calm spreading out to encompass all who could use it. The need would be great.

Chris and Ellen's world changed rapidly. Sequestered in their apartment, Mary gave them a crash course on what to expect. It sounded familiar but as Julie had always said, you can lead a horse to water but you can't make him drink. They hadn't been quite thirsty enough back then.

Chris whinnied and laughed at the looks he received.

"Are you all right?" Ellen asked.

"Yeah, I'm great," he said. "I'm a horse and I'm finally drinking. I'm really glad the water's still here for us."

Ellen shook her head. "Sometimes I just don't understand you. This is serious, Chris. It's hardly a time for riddles."

"Hey, El, it's a perfect time to laugh. Think about it! We've been experiencing all the things Julie and Dad talked about for a couple of years. We called them flaky behind their backs—with love, of course," he added. "Everything Mary and Emma are saying makes sense. Even if it gets wilder than it already is, we understand it now. Think of what life might be like in the next few years. It's like jumping from grade school to college in one giant leap. I think we've got a lot more to learn, Ellen."

"I love you so much, honey. Right now more than ever." Her eyes glistened with tears.

"Hey, don't do that," Chris pleaded.

"I'm okay. It's just been like a roller coaster ride the last couple of weeks."

Mary put her arm around Ellen. "Ellen needs to tell you about something that's been troubling her greatly." She looked at Ellen. "He needs to know about the lump."

"What is Mary talking about, Ellie? Is something wrong?"

Ellen was dumbfounded. "How did you know, Mary? I haven't told a soul."

"I guess it's a woman thing, ma'am. Go ahead, get it off your chest."

Ellen turned to Chris, her voice barely above a whisper. "I found a lump on my breast a couple of weeks ago. I knew you'd say to have surgery right away but I wasn't ready to make that decision. I've been so upset." Her eyes reflected her fear.

The color drained from Chris's face. He took her in his arms. "Oh, Ellie, why didn't you tell me? What can I do? You have to get rid of it!"

"There's nothing we can do right now. Just pray for me and be with me. I'll be okay. Actually, I'm glad Mary brought it up. It's a load off my back to finally be able to talk about it." She turned to Mary. "But how did you know, Mary?"

Mary just smiled.

"Angels do come in unexpected ways, don't they?" Ellen returned the smile.

~ ~ ~

The cave was cold but protected. Steve and his family were grateful to have found this safe haven, to have made it all in one piece. Whatever this thing was, it was right in their faces. They talked about the last few years and connected the dots; the stresses, mood swings, the pressure of not enough time. Pieces of the puzzle began to fall into place. Was it too late? They didn't think so or Steve wouldn't be in the cave right now. He'd be a pile of broken bones in the canyon below.

"Please tell us a story, Daddy," Mike asked. "Tell us one of your stories, okay?"

"Okay, tiger. Which one would you like?"

"Tell us about how we got here, Dad," Jesse said.

Megan laughed. "Have you forgotten about climbing the cliff already, Jess?"

"Oh Mommy, not that one!" Jesse said with a touch of exasperation. "I mean about when you wanted a baby and had to wait until we were ready and everything."

"Ah, *that* one." Megan smiled. The kids never tired of hearing how much they were wanted or how she and Steve had talked and sung to them during their nine-month incubation. It had taken so long to get pregnant and then to be blessed with twins was truly a miracle. Mike and Jesse loved being the leading characters in their own family mystery story.

"Gather round, guys. Let's get comfortable," Steve said.

They snuggled together, Rusty getting his love scratches on whatever part of his body was closest. It didn't matter to him as long as all his people were there. Peace and contentment reigned in the desolate cave in the Rockies, in the midst of the most incredible changes ever witnessed in the universe.

~ ~ ~

Things were not as peaceful elsewhere. Terror was rampant in cities, with entire city blocks burning out of control as firefighters tried to pump water from dry hydrants. Police barricaded themselves in precinct houses, afraid of the howling mobs outside. Every gun shop had been ransacked and armed gangs prowled the dark streets, looting, raping, and killing at will, unchecked by safeguards that had previously held society together. Everything unraveled in a matter of hours. It was as though mankind had lost control and was coming apart from fear, an awesome catalyst.

There were, however, pockets of peace, communities that had come together through spiritual guidance, but there was little anyone could do. The dark side was too invasive.

The buildup hadn't happened overnight. Removing prayer from schools took away the only connection to God that many children had. They were given a great deal of latitude both in schools and at home. Some parents even became afraid of their own kids as boundaries were challenged and control lost. Children of all ages often showed a lack of respect for others as well as themselves. TV, movies, music and commercials went over the edge in violence and sex, hypnotizing young minds and lowering the standards of what was acceptable.

Terrorism swept through the world, devastating countries and causing untold loss of life. Anger and rage at the assault on humanity was felt throughout the world. The frustration of an unseen enemy made people crazy. Our secure nation, thought Julie, our trusted security system is gone. We took our freedom for granted and it has been violated in the worst way.

The darkness went from bad to worse when the media began escalating terror to new heights, creating its own phenomena of mass hysteria. It was the climax of years of searching out the sensationalism, vying for the best ratings, sucking in the audience that had become numb to the horrific news being fed to them with their meals and before bed every night. There was no individuality, no independent thinking, especially on TV. Few dared to be different or to think differently, to create their own reality. If the media said the world would implode, that was it.

The violence in the streets, the gang wars, the shootings, the blood and guts, and death fed on itself. Panic swept across the continents. Mad Cow and Hoof and Mouth diseases ushered in a whole new lifestyle for mankind, but it was just the beginning. AIDS had wiped out half of Africa but it was minor compared to later plagues. Economic fear was the straw that broke the camel's back. People around the world quite simply gave up. They chose not to take part in what was coming, preferring to end it all with drugs, a bullet to the head or by whatever means available. Darkness overshadowed the light.

The jolt of wind brought Julie out of her deep trance. An awareness of a world in chaos lingered in her thoughts, and her body shook as the reality of the Shift overwhelmed her. The family was safe—challenged but safe. Refocusing her thoughts, she tried to connect with Jon regarding a more personal and urgent concern.

Julie directed her energies to him. At first there was nothing, static on the line so to speak. She released trying to control the cosmic airways. It worked.

"Mom, is that you? Have you blown away yet?"

"Jon! I'm so glad I reached you. It's howling here but I think we're secure. How about you?"

"This is wild. The good news is that the streets have been swept clean of dirt, dust, and looters. I'm sitting in the basement, away from the windows, just in case. I'm okay, staying cool. Been doing some writing, sort of documenting what I'm feeling. Who knows? Maybe someone will want to read about this crazy thing someday. We got a hell of a jolt here a while ago. I don't know what it was but something sure happened somewhere."

"We got it, too, but we're okay." Julie phrased her next question carefully. "Jon, would you tune into Jeannie and tell me if you sense anything … um … unusual? I'm a little concerned."

"Hang on. Let me focus." There was a short pause. "She's getting close, isn't she. I can feel the vibrations. I connected with the incoming soul and it knows exactly when it will arrive. Could be real soon."

"I knew it. Damn! I think she's sensing it. When I was looking for diversions I thought of games. You know, charades, Pictionary, Scrabble. *Not* the birth of a baby, for Pete's sake!"

"Have you forgotten something, Mom? Like maybe everything happens for a reason? What an incredible time to have a child, just when the world is in the process of rebirthing. That's awesome! You've got plenty of guides and teachers around. Ask them to find you an obstetric angel. Do your hands-on healing, a little hypnosis. Sterilize some things and you're on your way."

"Jon, you're an angel. And you're right, of course."

"Seriously, Mom, she couldn't be in better hands if something does happen. I'll send my energies, too. All you have to do is call."

"Thanks. I feel better now. Take care of yourself, Jon. There's nothing anyone can really do at this point except send out prayers and peace. And you, my good man, are in my thoughts and my heart."

"Bye for now, Mom. If you feel a nudge, open up and I'll come for a visit."

"Will do. I love you."

"I love you, too."

The kitchen was a mess, the result of a massive food search by a hungry mob. They were clustered around the fire in the living room, talking softly about what was happening. Joey, his hands resting on Jean's stomach, was feeling the baby move in the womb. He looked up at Julie with a glowing smile.

"Grammy, the baby's hitting me. It feels funny," he giggled. Suddenly looking quite serious, he announced, "I've been talking to her."

Jean glanced at Jerry. "We don't know whether it's a boy or a girl, Joey. We won't know until it's born."

"Well, *I* know. But I won't tell anyone," he whispered.

"How about some music, Dave?" Julie said, changing the subject. "I doubt any of us, certainly not all of us at the same time, have ever been without TV or a radio so let's make our own entertainment."

"Yeah, Dave," Bill chimed in. "Let's do a repeat performance." He smiled, remembering the last concert.

Dave picked up his guitar, strummed a few notes, and sang out, *You Are My Sunshine*. The harmony of the music and a family drawn together in crisis filled the room. Julie captured the moment in her heart and wrapped it in love for safekeeping. This was one memory she never wanted to forget.

Chapter Fourteen

The gale-force wind died down overnight, replaced by a thick blanket of fog that crept into the valleys. By morning, the forest, the house, and the nerves of those inside had relaxed somewhat.

Julie put on her old work boots and heavy jacket and slipped out the door, Max and Sandy on her heels. Fifty feet down the path she heard the door open behind her and Joey ran to her side.

He grabbed her hand. "Grammy, please, can I go with you? I wanna see the animals." He had dressed himself in a hurry; his clothes were backwards and inside out. He carried his boots that were "just like Grammy's."

"Sure, honey." She gave him a hug and helped him with his boots.

Hand in hand, they headed down the gravel path. The dense fog was cold, damp, disorienting, mysterious and totally out of place in the dry air of Colorado.

Julie could barely see the outline of the barn just 200 feet away. The dogs were curiously subdued. The whole world was silent on this day of mists, of increasing darkness leading to total darkness. She felt as though she had entered a fantasy movie, a mystical dream world where she was floating a foot above Mother Earth but connected to it at the same time.

"Grammy, what's happening?" Joe whispered, his face filled with wonder. "It's spooky, like being in an airplane and going through a cloud."

"I'm not sure, Joey. I guess it's another gift for us on our road to harmony in the world, something new for us to experience. We have to trust that God knows what He's doing. A lot of damage we've created on our planet is being repaired and I guess whatever is occurring today needs to be done in secret."

Joey nodded in agreement. There was a skip to his walk but he stayed close and held her hand tightly.

Julie lit the lantern hanging from a beam. The rich aroma of hay and animals filled her nostrils as she made the rounds, talking, whispering, patting and comforting the horses, goats, cats, and chickens. Joey mimicked her every move. The animals were hungry but very subdued considering what they'd been through. She opened the doors so the horses could get some exercise but after venturing out twenty feet, they returned to their stalls, uneasy, waiting for something unseen.

She brushed them until their coats gleamed, and spread fresh hay for their beds. The goats delighted Joey. She milked Daisy Mae and squirted a little in Joey's hand. She laughed when he wrinkled his nose after a tentative taste. They gathered eggs and she found herself thinking of her childhood summers in Maine.

"Remember the stories I've told you about the island in Maine and my Grandfather's big old barn, Joey? It was filled with such wonderful things to explore and touch and play with."

"Tell me again, Grandma!"

"Well, it had a great hay loft and my grandfather kept his rickety old car on the main floor. It was *really* old. I used to pretend I was driving on wonderful trips around the world. But the best part of the barn was Molly, the cow. There wasn't anything unusual about her except when Uncle Clarence milked her. He was a pretty big man and looked funny perched on his little three-legged stool. He'd put a bucket under Molly's heavy bag of milk that mysteriously filled up every morning and evening."

"Just like Daisy Mae, Grammy. You milk her, too."

"That's right, Joey. Uncle Clarence had a cat named Fluff that sat patiently by the wall behind the cow, waiting for her treat. She'd open her mouth when Uncle Clarence shot a stream of milk at her but it went all over her face. Then she'd try to lick the milk off her whiskers and nose but that made her look cross-eyed."

Joey giggled. "Can I shoot some of Daisy Mae's milk at one of your cats?"

"Maybe next time we milk we can find a cat willing to get a milk bath. Our aim might not be as precise as Uncle Clarence's. But if you can get the cat to sit still, we'll give it a try."

"I'll do it. I bet I can!"

Julie gathered the eggs and milk and Joey called the dogs. She doused the lantern and they left the barn and its earthy aroma.

Fog still enveloped the land. Holding her grandson's hand felt good. She remembered the day she had introduced the joy of hugging a tree to him. The look in his eyes as he had wrapped his arms around the trunk of the old pine had moved her deeply.

"Grammy, can we hug a tree? Would that one be good to hug?" Joey asked, pointing to a good-sized aspen. Telepathy was a wondrous thing.

"Any and all trees are good to hug, Joey. Let's talk to it and ask it to pass on a message of thanks for hanging in with all the others."

And so they did.

~ ~ ~

They left their damp coats and boots in the mudroom, and Joey disappeared down the hall. Julie lit some candles in the kitchen and put a pot of water on the stove for coffee and oatmeal, grateful for the still usable propane.

Joey reappeared in the doorway, an apparition of a small angel without wings, dragging his matted brown bear by one arm. His eyes adjusted to the darkness and he ran to Julie with a grin. She scooped him up and gave him a big hug, and he returned the favor with a wet kiss. She plunked him down on a stool at the counter and offered him a banana. He growled like a monkey and collapsed in giggles. Julie laughed, too. It felt good.

Joey cocked his head to one side. "Grammy, is Aunt Jeannie going to have her baby today?"

"I guess it's possible. What made you think that?"

"Mister G talked to me this morning. He said that a lot of things are going to happen, and to be strong. I don't know what he meant. He said something about a baby. Was he talking about Aunt Jeannie?"

Julie thought for a moment. "You know, Joey, he could have meant a couple of things. But, yes, you are going to have a new cousin pretty soon. We'll be ready just in case, okay?"

"Sure, Grammy. Can I help?"

"For now just give Aunt Jeannie lots of love and peace. That's what she needs most." Actually, thought Julie, what she doesn't need is for the baby to come early.

Joey folded his hands and did whatever it was he needed to do to send his energies to his aunt. Julie had no doubt it would have the desired effect.

It surprised her how quickly she had become accustomed to and accepted the changing physical manifestations. Dizziness and nausea still swept over her when she moved too quickly, and the tingling on and under her skin felt like a small charge of energy through a not quite grounded electrical cord. She felt occasional blood rushes, almost like the hot flashes of old, followed by chills. Yes, no doubt about it. Her DNA was being altered.

Chapter Fifteen

Rusty loudly proclaimed the beginning of a new day, bringing all four cave dwellers to their feet with a jolt. All except Megan, who could enjoy eight hours of sleep regardless of earth changes and upside down world events.

"Holy mackerel!" Steve said.

"Wow! Daddy, what is that?" Mike asked.

Jesse was awe struck. "It's a fantasy land, Daddy, like in a dream. Mommy, come see this! I can't see anything!"

That brought Megan out of her sleeping bag. She found her men, including the dog, standing in a row, looking out over, or rather into, an impenetrable world of mist and clouds.

"What is it, Steve? It looks like the fog at the ocean."

"The ocean's a long way away. Maybe we're in a low cloud. But it's even different from that I think. How do you feel this morning, honey?"

"Tired. I'm very tired. I'm going back to bed. Wake me when it clears up." Megan headed back to her sleeping bag.

"Hey, Megan, wait a minute! I'm serious. How do you feel? I mean, I feel weird. There's something strange happening inside me. It's okay but is it just me?"

"I feel funny, too, Daddy," Jesse said. "I feel prickly and like I can almost fly," he added, wonder in his voice.

"Me, too!" Mike said, not one to be left out of anything.

"Well, don't get any ideas about flying here, guys," Steve warned. "It's a long way down. You know, it could get pretty cold with this fog. Let's get some firewood. Megan, you can get the candles ready. It'll be like a very different kind of camping trip, right kids?"

"Yeah, Dad," Mike said. "But you'll have to get the wood. I think I'll stay here and make sure Mom's okay.

"Good idea, son. And you'll need Jesse's help. We wouldn't want Mom to get in any trouble," he said, winking at his groggy wife.

Mary and Emma tried to second guess where Ellen might have put dishes and food. They wanted to prepare breakfast for their rescuers and had made some headway when Chris appeared in the doorway.

"Is it morning?" he mumbled. His eyes were puffy, still half asleep.

"Yes, sir," Mary said. "Sometime during the night the wind stopped. It's been real strange out there ever since. You might want to take a look."

Chris shuffled to the window and lifted a slat on the mini-blinds. "It's foggy. I see fog."

"Yes, but it's something else."

"What do you mean, 'something else'? It's fog. I can see it." He was puzzled. Morning wasn't the time to argue. Hadn't they been in fog before?

"I'll be back in a few minutes," he said, sounding bewildered. "Some of the stuff in the freezer might still be okay. Help yourself to whatever you can find. Just save the chocolate milk for me. You'll like me better if you do."

~ ~ ~

San Francisco had survived so far, at least what was left of it after the big quake that fractured the west coast. The absolute quiet awakened Jon from his dreams. He'd had a busy out-of-body night. A good day's night, he called it. He had physically bi-located during the night, something that happened frequently. Last night he had gone to the hospital for young cancer patients again. They'd been exposed to plenty of fear with their disease, and many had been through near-death experiences or were close to transitioning now. Most had accepted spiritual phenomena of some sort and welcomed Jon's appearance without question.

He left his temporary basement bedroom and climbed up the stairs to his apartment. The wind had smashed his picture window; the place looked like a tornado had swept through it. With an old blanket from Mexico and a hammer and nails, he created a colorful wall hanging that would keep the draft down. Grabbing a broom, he hummed and danced a Mexican Hat Dance around the pile of glass.

It wasn't a cold time of year but the fog was intense. Strangely, it didn't smell of salt air. It was a dry fog. He shrugged, found some crackers and cheese dip and his notepad, and continued his journal of the Photon experience. Cocking his head to one side, he became aware of the intense silence. The familiar sounds of the city had disappeared.

"Julie! Julie, where are you? Julie!" Jerry called, stumbling through the dark.

"I'm here. What is it, Jerry? What's the matter?"

"It's Jeannie. She's hurting. It's the baby. I think it might be coming!"

"Take it easy, Jerry. Go back to her. I'll be right there. Joey, you stay here and finish your breakfast, okay? I want to hear more about your Mister G when I get back."

Julie grabbed a candle and followed Jerry, a shiver of apprehension running down her spine.

Jean was curled up in bed, very pale and more than a little frightened. "Julie, I think the baby's coming. I keep getting these cramps and my belly gets so tight. I didn't want to say anything but they're getting worse. It's too soon. What should I do?"

"First of all, relax, honey. Lots and lots of women have been through this before, including me. We'll take good care of you and you'll be just fine. The more you fight it, the more it'll hurt and the longer it will take. The idea is to let the muscles loosen so your baby can have a quick and pleasant trip down that long tunnel into the new world. You've learned the breathing techniques and I'll help you with hypnosis." She turned to Jerry. "Time to get yourself together, my friend. She needs you to help her, to guide her like you learned in class. Have you checked to see how far apart the contractions are?"

"I'm not sure. I think maybe five or ten minutes."

Julie smiled. "To a woman in labor, the difference between five and ten minutes is enormous, Jerry." Men just don't have a clue, she thought. "How about trying to time them for me? I think it'll be a while but I need to get some things together before whatever else is going to happen today starts happening." She turned to Jean. "Let's try a little visualization so you can get some rest. New mommies need all the rest they can get."

"Oh Julie, I'm so glad I'm here."

"So am I, honey, so am I."

Julie pulled a chair up to the bed. She fluffed the pillows and tucked in the blankets. A candle cast a soft glow as she began a hypnotic induction. She took Jeannie through the parts of her body, relaxing them one by one. A contraction interrupted the routine but this time Julie's soft voice and instructions made it easier.

Jeannie easily slipped into an alpha state. Julie gave her suggestions on ways to control the pain. They both talked to the baby, reassuring it that it was safe and loved, that they couldn't wait for it to arrive quickly and easily.

Jerry watched and listened but he could barely keep his eyes open. Julie made sure he wasn't unknowingly hypnotized, then left them in a relaxed state.

Her hands were shaking as she gathered everything she could think of that they might possibly need, going quietly from closet to kitchen to bedroom with blankets, sheets, scissors, even a needle and thread. She had lots of candles, thank goodness.

The changing electromagnetics had played havoc with all the clocks and watches. Not one was working right. They'd have to guess on timing. The days of schedules and doing everything by the clock were gone for good. If you're hungry, eat. If you're sleepy, sleep. A whole new time-space continuum was coming. It made much more sense.

Julie stopped by her bedroom where Dave was deep in his dream world. She gave him a kiss on his peaceful brow. The corner of his mouth twitched into a smile. She'd need him well rested later on.

She checked on Jean again, then rejoined Joey, who was happily stuffing the last of her secret supply of sugar donuts into his mouth.

"Joey Cramer! What are you doing? How did you find those, for heaven's sake?"

He hung his head and looked up at her with guilty eyes, a sugary telltale ring around his pouting mouth.

She put on her best scowling look but it wasn't working. Biting her lip, she quickly stuck her head in a cabinet to look for something—anything—to stifle a giggle that threatened to erupt.

"What time is it?" Bill said in a half stupor, groping his way to the smell of coffee.

"I haven't a clue, Bill. It's probably morning since you're up, but I can guarantee that nothing today will seem normal. How are you feeling?"

"Kinda weird."

"Me, too. Can you deal with it?"

"Yup. I could deal better with a hot cup of coffee, though."

"How are Erica and Kathy? Any problems?" Julie asked, filling a mug.

"No. Still asleep. "

"Good. I'm going to need lots of help later."

"Why? What's up, besides this Shift thing?"

"Jean's in labor," Julie said.

"You're kidding! She can't have a baby *now!*"

"Sweetheart, she can have it any old time her body wants to. Have you forgotten so soon?"

"No. Some things you never ever forget. How far along is she? When will it happen? What can I do?" He was awake now.

"That's anyone's guess. She's about five to ten minutes apart, according to Jerry. It could be three hours or three days. She's resting. Jerry's with her. You can be a lot of help to him with this,

Bill. As a birth assistant, no one's better than you. Basically, we all need to live in the moment and take it as it comes."

"I'll go say hi and see what I can do."

"Thanks, honey. Come get me if you need me."

Carrying a flickering candle that created ghost-like images on the walls, Kathy walked Jean around the house and guided her breathing with each contraction. A nervous Jerry was getting instructions from Bill. Grandpa Dave kept Joey in a discussion about cars and trucks, a strong mutual interest. Julie had played a lot of roles in her life but midwife was not one of them.

The contractions were getting closer and stronger. This was Jean's first child and, as the pain increased, Jeannie had no idea how much more intense it would get.

A surge of different energy raced through Julie's body and she grabbed the counter to steady herself. Glancing around the kitchen, her heart skipped a beat. The plastic container of water that was there a minute ago had disappeared, leaving a large puddle on the floor. A quick look around confirmed that many plastic items had simply disappeared. Anything plastic "not used with love and for the good of all" could disintegrate, she'd been told by Spirit. "Plastic used to harm Mother Earth and her inhabitants will disassemble within seconds … learn to detach from things, be able to release them in love. It shall be given to you according to your beliefs."

The Styrofoam cups have turned to dust even as I stand here, Julie thought, amazed. She had long ago switched to natural fabric in her clothes, which, fortunately, seemed to be holding together. She knew beyond a shadow of a doubt that her belief in the love and protection of God was inviolate. Whatever disappeared was for the good of all. Nevertheless, she turned and quickly made her way to the office. Her computer was still standing. No power, but it was there. She wondered if the IRS would be in deep trouble. The possibility made her smile.

Kathy appeared in the doorway looking puzzled. "Julie, Erica's diapers aren't here. Have you seen them?"

"Now you know what Spirit considers expendable on Planet Earth," Julie answered.

Some conveniences of the modern world would be but a memory. She wondered if the landfills would become sinkholes when the zillions of empty milk and water cartons, not to mention soap containers, all turned to dust. She visualized a large bubble of love and pure white light encircling the house and barn. She had always felt protected in her home but not invulnerable.

"Grandma, Grandma! I didn't do it, honest, I didn't do it!"

Joey looked pretty guilty for someone who 'didn't do it,' Julie thought.

"Do what, honey?

"The potato chips. I was feeding some to Max and Sandy and now they're all over the floor. I don't know what happened."

Lucky dogs, Julie thought. Too bad the chips didn't disappear along with the bag.

Chapter Sixteen

The family gathered in the living room. Dave had placed a mattress near the fire for Jean. It had been a long day and promised to be an even longer night. Her contractions were regular and often. Candles cast enough light to take the edge off the intense darkness.

The pressure hit them all at the same time. It felt as though gravity was pressing them into the earth. Everyone appeared to move in slow motion. Julie wondered if her neighbors were frightened and what was happening to the rest of her family. They were cut off from the world. What was it she had read? "You'll feel as though you might have died but they forgot to tell you." What else is coming that pushes us to *that* point? The word "TRUST' exploded in her head with a vengeance and she answered with, "Peace. Be Still."

Between the plywood-covered windows and the mist that blocked out the light, it was dark and getting colder. Dave tried to keep the fire going in the fireplace but the pressure seemed to be suffocating the flames, too. Julie worried that the flickering candles would go out. That would be a problem since the flashlights didn't work anymore.

Jerry held his wife in his arms, breathing with her through the contractions. Everyone breathed with her, which made her laugh once she caught her breath. Julie ran Reiki energy through her hands into Jean's energy field, allowing it to go where it was needed most.

It was more comfortable for everyone to be lying down and not fighting the gravity pull. It was so dark and the wind was building up again, whistling around the windows and the corners of the house.

The pressure, the sense of being pushed into the floor, slowly increased. Julie wondered how heavy it would get before it reversed. It would reverse; it had to. It was a double whammy for Jeannie who was experiencing pressure inside as well as out. She was making progress but it was taking too damn long.

The contractions were tough. Julie worked with Jean, trying to keep her in a hypnotic alpha state, reminding her to use the 'pain box' and turn the dial down when a contraction started. It helped but she was getting very tired. Jerry reassured her as much as he could.

"You know," Julie said, trying to ease the tension, "this child is truly blessed to be coming into the world at this time. I'm sure there's a special reason none of us know. I would guess the baby has a message for all of us. We just don't know what it is yet." She brushed the hair from Jean's face. "How are you doing, honey?"

Jean's voice seemed to come from far away. "I'm wonderful. Really. The contractions—they're not as painful, just a lot of pressure that actually feels good. Something has changed, Julie. I don't know what. Ohhh, here we go again."

"Breathe, Jeannie. Stay with me," Jerry pleaded.

"Dave," Julie said, "we've got to have more light. Can you see if the fire will start again? Maybe a candle or something?"

"I'll see what I can do."

"Don't step on anyone!"

"Don't worry. I wouldn't dare stand up. Bill, help me find the matches. Kathy, keep the kids close to you so we don't bump into them."

"We're okay. Erica's with me. Joey? Where are you?"

"Here, Mom," he whispered. "Shhh. I'm helping Aunt Jeannie."

"What? What are you doing? I don't want you to get lost in the dark."

"I'm putting my hands on her head like Grammy does. I want to help her."

"Jean? Is it okay, whatever he's doing? Do you want him to stop?" Kathy asked.

"No. No, please don't stop." Jean whispered. "I didn't know what it was, but I feel the most wonderful heat inside my body. It feels so relaxing, just a beautiful feeling. If Joey's responsible for that, he's got himself a job. Ohhh, it's coming again. It hurts!"

"I found them! I've got the matches!" Bill shouted.

"Great!" Dave said. "I found the fireplace. Where are you? Follow my voice." He rumpled up paper to stuff under the wood. The sound was reassuring.

"Okay," Bill said. "Here we go."

He struck a match. It flickered and went out. It took five tries before the paper was flaming. "I think I know how cavemen felt about fire. It kept them warm and they could cook, but I wonder if they thought of it in terms of light. I can almost see you guys." They all felt the relief. The pressure began to lift.

Jean began pushing and straining. Her breathing had changed. In between pants, she kept saying, "I've got to push, I can't help it—ohhh."

"Julie, do something!" Jerry shouted.

"Take it easy, Jerry. She needs you to stay with her breathing. The baby's started down the birth canal. It can take a while. Jean, I need to see what's going on. Dave, get me a candle."

Julie was bluffing. She'd never done this before. She didn't even know what she was looking for. Silently she prayed, "Dear Lord, please give me a hand here. Any guidance will be much appreciated." Carefully, she lifted the blanket.

Chapter Seventeen

Megan had conserved their meager supply of dried foods and fruit as well as she could. She felt like a pioneer, stranded in a cave in the wilderness, trapped in a hostile environment, cut off from the rest of the world. It was almost a game, a deadly serious one. She sent a steady stream of prayers to the angels, especially now that she was sure at least Steve had one around. No one could sleep, not even Rusty. It was pitch black.

Megan tried to sit up but felt incredibly heavy. Feeling around for a candle and some matches, she managed to get a flame started. Creeping to the cave entrance, she felt as though she was living a dream. There was nothing, literally nothing. Not a star, no moon, no shadows. Just black nothingness. She shivered and inched her way back into her sleeping bag and cuddled up next to her husband and children to wait.

They felt so terribly alone in their isolated cave. When the candle snuffed out, they thought they might, too. The pressure was intense. Huddled together, they kept each other warm, telling stories to the boys, trying to make an adventure, a game, out of the experience. Steve was so busy reassuring his family, that he actually made a shift of his own. He believed what he was saying. He didn't feel fear, just concern over the safety of his loved ones.

He wondered what their families were doing, who was where, if all were okay. If they were even alive.

Swallowing hard, he reassured his family. "This, too, will pass. We've got each other and we've got love. That's the most important thing in the world. Peace, be still. We're not alone." He knew it was true.

Jon rarely stayed in his body at night anymore. He found himself in a big building he hadn't visited before. The complex was filled with children and a few adults. A sign over the doorway said, "Home Away From Home," a shelter where orphaned children were cared for, children who had survived the massive earth changes. There were several such communities. He knew God was watching over the kids who hadn't made conscious or even unconscious decisions to leave the Third Dimension before the Shift. During a time of trauma, and this Shift certainly qualified for that, surrogate parents could use all the help they could get.

He saw the hazy outlines of angels, beings of light, and he had the feeling he was walking between dimensions. He was lucid enough to realize he had once again left his body in a sleep state and was "on assignment."

He began his sojourn through the rooms, watching for the restless, the frightened. By holding their hands, he was able to bring them peace and reassurance that their world was still intact. The children talked about being in total darkness, unable to see their hands in front of their eyes, but he could see them.

Jon always experienced life in a different way than anyone else. He had no fears, few inhibitions, and a sense of joy and excitement in his being that others envied but few could emulate.

He "heard" the warning in his head, something about protecting the silver cord, and was instantly back in his body before the Shift. He knew he was in familiar territory but couldn't see a thing. "Man!" he had exclaimed, "this is frigging *dark!*"

He had wanted to tune in to his mother but decided to heed the warning and ride it out. Something was happening, no doubt about that. He felt the energy changes taking place within his body and tried to analyze the sensations. There was no fear, only concern for his family, his friends. Some would make it. Some would not. He'd see them all again ... somehow.

He really had to work at staying grounded when the pressure neared its peak. The hurricane wind lessened when the pressure set in and slowly dropped to stillness. It was cold, very cold. The Zero Point was coming. This was an outrageous event and he had no intention of missing a moment of it.

That still small voice within spoke to him again, the one that repeated the word "trust" so often. The guidance was short but profound: "Become one with what you are becoming."

He relaxed in the darkness. Going deeply within, he found his inner peace and waited for the next installment. Soon he would check on the rest of the family. But for now he simply rested in the arms of his Guardian Angel.

Chris and Ellen were highly motivated to find their spirituality, making agreements to always do the right thing—prayers that surface when faced with life-threatening events or circumstances that can't be comprehended or explained.

Mary and Emma explained the mysterious occurrences, not only in the apartment, but also around the world. Chris wondered how they knew so much. They were so aware, so at peace. When he had opened his eyes to what he thought was morning, he had panicked. He couldn't see the little green light on the smoke detector that had always reminded him of a tiny flying saucer. He awoke to a black void. Heart pounding, he'd made his way slowly down the hall, feeling disoriented, lost in a black fear.

His guests were awake and talking softly to each other, or to someone he couldn't see. They heard him stumble as he reached the living room.

"Chris? Is that you?" Emma asked.

"Yeah. But I can't see you. I can't see anything! What's happening?" The wind picking up again didn't help.

"Don't be afraid," said Mary. "The Lord is with us; our angels are with us. We've been protected so far and we'll continue to be."

She was so reassuring that his heart rate slowed and he felt better immediately. Bless these wonderful new friends, he thought.

"We're on our path to paradise. Thank you, Lord!" she said with heartfelt emotion.

"Paradise, huh?" said Chris. "Well, I'd like to see the path *I'm* moving on! I've got to find a candle or something."

"The easiest way to find your path and travel it in safety is to trust in God and trust in yourself," Mary said. "Fill your heart with so much love there's no room for fear. Think of all the blessings of your life and how much love you can send to everyone in the world. No limitations because of race or color or creed. Love and trust. Peace, be Still. Let that be your mantra for the day, for your life, and you'll be just fine. Now get your candle and go to your wife. She has even more fear than you right now. She needs you. Bless you."

How had this simple woman become so wise? Chris wondered, and realized he had just made a judgment. How did he know whether she was simple or not? Maybe she was an angel or something. We're *all* equal, he reminded himself. What's on the outside means nothing. It's nothing but a shell, a house we use while we're living a life on earth. Who we really are goes with us when we die. We get to *choose* whether to come back to earth again or just stay and work on the other side. Other side of what, he wondered.

Then he did something he hadn't done in a long time. A prayer formed in his heart for his wife. "Please, God, please take care of Ellen. Make the lump in her breast go away. I couldn't bear to go on without her."

Chris was well aware that without Mary and Emma, he and Ellen might not have made it through. The comfort and knowledge they shared kept him from spiraling into panic. He wondered if he'd ever get to see his family again.

When the pressure began and the candles had blown out, Ellen had gotten pretty upset. He tried to put on a brave front but he knew it was a facade. Mary encircled them with her comforting arms, reminding them how privileged they were to have been chosen to live through the greatest adventure on earth in thousands of years.

"You'll be able to manifest anything you need just by thinking it. You can travel to other places without cars or planes," she added.

"Wait a minute, Mary," Chris said, "you're making this up, right?"

"No, my children, this we believe to be true."

His head was swimming. He knew one thing for sure. There were no color barriers that day, nor would there ever be, anywhere, ever again. They rested in the black of night, waiting for time to pass, for life to begin again.

Chapter Eighteen

The knock on the door made them all jump. "It's just the wind," Dave said, his heart skipping a beat. It came again. Knock, knock, knock.

"That was not the wind, Dave," Julie said. "There's someone at the door. But who in God's name would be out in this?" It was pitch black out, the wind was howling, the pressure was still intense.

Dave had included a long cotton rope in their supplies, a lifeline to guarantee that if anyone had to venture out, they could find their way back again. He quickly tied one end around his waist and gave the other end to Bill. Although the small fire cast faint shadows, its illumination didn't reach very far. He carefully crept in the direction of the front door.

"Who could even find this place in the dark?" Kathy asked.

"I haven't a clue," Julie said. "But it's hardly the time for visitors. Breathe, Jeannie, and push when you get that urge. Hang in there, baby. You're doing fine."

"Ohhhh!" Jean groaned, panting and pushing.

Julie had a gut feeling that something wasn't going quite right but she reassured Jean that all was well.

Joey was still standing at his aunt's head, his hands resting gently on her forehead, eyes closed. "Someone's come to help Aunt Jeannie. Mister G sent him."

"Well, thank Mister G for us," Jerry said. "We could use a little help." That and a buck might buy a cup of coffee, he thought to himself.

A gust of wind followed the door opening and voices could be heard. Retracing his rope trail, Dave cautiously crawled back to the group. The stranger walked as though he could see in the dark.

"I apologize for intruding at a time like this," he said, his voice deep and soothing. "The transition process is challenge enough without also dealing with childbirth. I can explain how I happened to be nearby later if you wish, but I received a clear and urgent message to come here to help. I know you don't know me but I've delivered many, many babies. I'm here to offer my services if you'd like them."

They all breathed a sigh of relief. For reasons she couldn't possibly have explained, Julie trusted this stranger out of the darkness.

"Jeannie, is it okay if he gives us a hand?" Julie asked. "I'm right here but he says he knows what he's doing, which is more than I can say. It might be a good idea."

"Hey, no way," Jerry said. "I don't want some stranger messing with my wife."

"Easy, Jerry," said Dave. "I'm sure it's—"

Through clenched teeth, Jean moaned. "Just … get … the baby … out … please!"

"I'll try to get some more light for you, another candle. What else do you need?" Bill asked the stranger.

"Nothing. I can see perfectly," he said, settling down at the end of the mattress. There seemed to be a glow about him.

Jeannie was straining and pushing hard. Everyone in the room felt her pain.

"Jean," the stranger encouraged, "you're doing a splendid job. It won't be long. Relax and do what feels natural to you."

He gently placed his hands on her stomach. They were warm and Jean felt herself relax in spite of the advancing contraction.

"Here are blankets, sheets, scissors, string. And I found a nose dropper to use for a syringe, if that'll work," Julie said. "What else do you need that we might have?"

"Nothing. This is perfect. What an incredibly wonderful time to bring a child into the world. Your family is blessed and so is this child." His voice was deep and calming. "Jean, let's help the baby along and do some really big pushes. Visualize your child slipping easily out of the birth canal, see it happening, know it's happening. You have the power to manifest that right now. Do it for the baby's sake."

She trusted and pushed. Julie was aware of Joey's hands still on the top of Jean's head. His eyes were closed and his lips moved soundlessly, as though talking to an invisible someone. Bill was watching his son closely, too.

Jerry gripped Jeannie's hand and Julie held the other as the stranger attended to his work. With a final push and groan, the baby was delivered into the visitor's gentle, waiting arms. He smiled and carefully placed the child on the mother's tummy. "Jean and Jerry, you are the parents of a beautiful daughter." Soft blue energy radiated from the baby's body. "She is a child of the new Blue Ray, an Indigo child born to make a difference in the new world."

Jean sobbed with relief and joy. Everyone hugged in the darkness, everyone but Julie. Her eyes were focused on the hole in the middle of the baby's back. She noted the child's limp legs. The blood left her face and she began to tremble uncontrollably. Her eyes met the stranger's in the dim candlelight. He nodded in confirmation of the birth defect. Julie was stunned. History was repeating itself.

The visitor from nowhere carefully cut and tied the cord, wrapped a soft blanket around the baby and held her for a moment. His eyes were closed and he whispered, "Little child of God, beautiful newborn soul, we welcome you to this world, this family. You will be loved and nurtured throughout your new venture in the Fifth Dimension. Bless you, dear one." He then handed her to her mother who tenderly placed the baby to her breast.

The stranger quietly went about the business of finishing up. It had been a gentle release. Jean had not torn and the placenta was delivered easily and completely. When he was finished, he stood up. The glow remained around him.

"This little angel," he said, looking at Julie, "is a perfect soul and a very gifted child. She has much to teach your family and the world. Her body has a problem, one that you're familiar with." He turned to Jeannie. "She has what you call spina bifida. But you must trust in God that she's perfect in every way … because she is."

Jeannie gasped. "I don't understand. What are you saying? She *is* perfect! I know she is!"

"What the hell are you talking about, man?" Jerry yelled. "You're scaring the hell out of us. You come in here, a stranger, and now you tell me there's something wrong with my kid? What did you do to it?"

Dave jumped up and put his arms around Jerry. "Easy. Take it easy. He didn't do anything. Just calm down. Your wife and daughter need you now more than ever, Jerry."

Julie shook her head to clear the painful memories. She put her hands on either side of Jean's face and turned it toward her. "Jeannie, look at me. Your daughter is perfect. Whatever is happening, it's God's will. Everything happens for a reason. It took me a long time to learn that from my baby but it's more important than you know to trust in God right now. Look at me, Jeannie. Do you understand what I'm saying? *She is a perfect being.* You must let go of fear *now*. Jeannie, do you hear me?"

Jean's eyes were full of pain. She answered with a slow blink.

The stranger knelt beside her. Gently he placed one hand on the baby's head and the other on the mother. He closed his eyes for a moment. His voice was quiet and soothing. "You and your baby are going to be fine. God is with you. Trust in love."

Jean looked deeply into his eyes. "I know. I do."

The man stood and reached out to Jerry but it was more than Jerry could stand. Wrenching out of Dave's grip, he ran for the door, stumbling over furniture and swearing. It slammed shut as he disappeared into the dark, cold and windy night.

"Jerry!" Jeannie screamed.

"Let him go," said the stranger. "He needs to be alone to deal with having what he considers an imperfect child. Jerry's angry—with God, with himself, with the world. Everyone must work through their own fears in their own way. It's important for your energy to be here for your daughter and yourself, Jean. You're surrounded in love. Your family will take care of you. Do you understand?"

And once again, she nodded. "Yes. Yes, I do."

She and the baby, and even Joey, were wrapped in something special, an invisible cocoon of light. The stranger communicated with them on a level Julie had not yet reached but she was awed by what she felt.

Recovering her composure, she reached out her hands to him. "Thank you for all you've done. I don't know how you were sent here but we'll be forever grateful. Will you stay with us? We have room and food. We'd be honored to have you join us."

"Thank you. I appreciate your kindness. But I have other work to do. I must leave now."

"But you can't leave now," Bill said. "It's nasty out there."

"It's only nasty if you believe it is. I can see perfectly well and the wind doesn't bother me. I do appreciate your concern."

He walked to Dave and took his hand. "Take good care of your family, David. They need your strength and your calm spirit." He kissed Jean on the forehead. "You are and will be a perfect mother for this little angel." He kissed the baby on the top of her head. "Have a wonderful life, my precious one."

He reached for Joey, who quickly wrapped his small arms around the stranger's neck. "Joey, it's good to see you again. We have a lot of work to do together some day. Say hello to Mister G for me the next time you see him," he said with a smile and a wink.

"I love you," Joey whispered.

He put Joey down. "There's another little one here I wish to give blessings to. You call her Erica. Yes, here she is." He lifted the smiling child into his arms. "What a wonderful life you're going to have, dear Erica. You have much to do, as all little children do." He kissed her forehead and handed her back to Kathy who was amazed. Erica, who usually complained loudly when touched by strangers, was smiling.

"God bless you all," the man said and walked into the darkness.

"Wait! We don't even know your name," Julie said.

"My name is not important. You'll see me again some day."

They heard the door open and close, felt the gust of wind ruffle their hair. They were speechless.

Jerry had run away at the worst possible time and the baby's birth defect had cast a pall over the group. But they knew without a doubt they had just been touched by an angel.

Chapter Nineteen

Darkness pervaded every nook and cranny of their cave. Jesse and Mike were jittery and keeping them occupied took all the ingenuity Megan and Steve had. They tied ropes around themselves and attached them to the children. The boys gathered small rocks to mark the cave opening.

There was a lump in Steve's throat and tears stung his eyes. He felt vulnerable, out-of-control. The internal physical vibrations had opened a door to emotions that had been locked up for a long time. It was bizarre. He wiped his eyes and groped for the bag of candles. He found them loose on the ground. The plastic container they had been in was gone. The discovery brought him back to the present. The bags holding the dried food had disappeared and the plastic cups were gone. He shrugged it off, and concentrated on living in the moment. It was all they had. They were survivors, Steve reminded himself, and this was simply one more notch on the tree of life. He smiled in the inky blackness.

Mary and Emma were excited about the anticipated possibilities of life after the Shift, and were willing to share what they knew. Their audience eagerly absorbed the information.

The sound of dripping water interrupted the discussion. "What the heck," Chris said, feeling around. His heart skipped a beat when he discovered the plastic bottles of water had disintegrated, leaving dripping puddles on the table beside the couch. Was this happening everywhere? Was the supermarket awash in water and milk?

Ellen gasped and Mary cleared her throat. "Oh, my goodness."

Chris struggled to light a candle. As the flame glowed on Mary's black shiny skin, he saw that her polyester dress was gone, and so was much of what had been under it. He saw the beauty of her body, the totality of who she was as she stood proud and radiant in her trust. And there was no embarrassment.

Ellen, whose nylon blouse had also done a disappearing act, cried out and quickly covered her breasts.

"Well, I guess things really are gonna be different from now on," Mary said handing Ellen a cotton sheet from the sofa bed. Her broad, generous laugh made them all feel more at ease.

The plastic mini-blinds had also disappeared, leaving the metal hangers and cotton pulls in place. Chris decided he wasn't sure whether he wanted to know what had or had not escaped this strange phenomenon. When he contemplated the amount of plastic in the world, the ramifications were tremendous.

He looked at his watch. The second hand was still.

Patience had never been Jon's strong suit. He quickly and easily manifested whatever it was he desired or needed, having mastered that skill as his belief system had grown. He had patience with the children he worked with and most adults. There were a few he wanted to shake, especially when they remained blocked and focused on a negative aspect of their lives. There was so much to do, see, feel, hear and experience through all the senses. Now with the expanded consciousness, his included, the waiting was just too much. It had taken thousands years to get to this point. Once the Shift occurred it would take thousands of years for the Photon energy to leave the solar system.

Material goods didn't get top billing with Jon. His interest and fascination was with untouchable things: telepathy, trans-locating, integrating past, future, and even present lives, being with ancestors and seeing the great Masters once again—*that* was worth waiting for. Time was moving too slowly for Jon, something he never thought he'd say again.

Some major adjustments were occurring in his body, although he couldn't tell just what they were. He wondered how 'his' kids in the hospitals would feel when they found themselves well and whole again. Because there was no doubt in his mind they would be. In fact, they'd probably think they'd died and gone to heaven. In a sense, they had. Their happiness brought tears to his eyes.

What Jon couldn't see was that the DNA in every cell of his body was shifting from two strands to twelve, ushering in the potential for full psychic sight, rejuvenation, even immortality. Those gifts would take time to manifest.

He sensed that something extraordinary had happened to his mother and the family. He didn't know what, but he didn't want to push himself to connect with them just yet. The energies were too new and unsettled.

The shock of the baby's birth had released Julie's tender memories of Danny. She felt the pain once again and marveled at Jean's calm acceptance. Suddenly the house shook as a loud jarring jolt knocked them flat. They all screamed and cried out. Then there was silence. Everything stopped. Nothing, absolutely nothing, was moving. *Everything* came to a halt. The fire in the fireplace was snuffed out, along with the candles. The wind quit blowing. Life itself seemed to hang in suspension. The pressure was intense as time literally stood still. The very air they breathed felt solid.

Julie wondered if they were dying, perhaps already had. It was an effort to speak. "Peace, be still," she murmured and the others took up the chant.

"Peace, be still. Peace, be still."

How long would it last? Seconds? Minutes? Forever? It felt like a lifetime.

Ever so slowly, life began again. The pressure lessened and they could breathe, although the air was still very dense. The darkness remained and it was cold, bone-chilling cold. They stretched their cramped muscles, unaware of how long they had been in a suspended state.

Julie cleared her throat and found her voice again. "Jeannie, are you and the baby okay?" she asked hoarsely.

"I think so."

"Kathy? Joey? Are you okay?" Bill asked.

"Yeah, I'm all right," Kathy answered, her voice a little shaky. "Joey? Are you okay, baby?"

"I'm okay, Mom. And I'm not a baby anymore!"

"I know, honey. I'm sorry. I sometimes forget you're so grown up."

"That's okay, Mom," Joey said, sounding different.

"Erica seems fine, too," Kathy said. "I can't believe how calm and quiet she's been since we got here. I just wish I could see something! I'm awfully glad we're all together."

Bill continued the roll call. "Mom, what just happened … and are you okay?"

"I'm fine," Julie said. "Oh, I hate the word 'fine.' It's so … nothing. What I'm really feeling is that something extraordinary just occurred, not just to us. To the world. I think we just experienced a big shift. *The* Shift. The Zero Point. Whatever is happening is so bizarre; we'll have to work at staying balanced. We and the earth are being shielded by this blackout and … um … well," she paused catching her breath, "I'm … ah … fine."

"That was more information than I asked for," Bill said, "but some things never change. Thank God you're one of them, Mom."

They all laughed, including Julie. The release of tension felt good.

Julie reached for Dave's hand. "Honey, how are you doing?"

"I'm fine." He gave Julie's hand a squeeze. "And I happen to like the word. So there."

"Way to go, Dave," Bill chuckled. "At least your personalities haven't changed. Jerry? Are you okay?" Then he remembered. They all remembered.

"Oh, no," Jeannie cried. "Where did he go? Is he all right? Please God, watch over my husband wherever he is," she pleaded, a sob catching in her throat. "Please help him to understand and bring him back to me."

The strange birth had kept the family so focused on Jean's well being, they hadn't been aware of their own physical and spiritual changes. Still in awe of the stranger's visit and all the events that had just taken place, they sat around the mattress, sensing the closeness and overwhelming love that encircled them. Although they couldn't see it, they all sent out sparkles of energy that were seen by entities in higher dimensions.

"Jeannie, do you have a name for your daughter yet?" Julie asked.

"Yes, but it's not the one we had originally picked out," she said, her voice unsteady. "She's my little angel, and I'm going to call her Angela. It's the only name she could possibly have."

"Perfect," Julie said.

In a sea of goose bumps and smiles, they knew they had crossed into the Fifth Dimension.

PART THREE

THE LIGHT

And I heard a great voice out of heaven saying," Behold, the tabernacle of God is with men, and he will dwell with them, and they shall be his people, and God himself shall be with them, and be their God.

"And God shall wipe away all tears from their eyes; and there shall be no more death, neither sorrow, nor crying, neither shall there be any more pain: for the former things are passed away."

And he that sat upon the throne said," Behold, I make all things new."' And he said unto me, "Write: for these words are true and faithful."

And he said unto me, "It is done. I am Alpha and Omega, the beginning and the end. I will give unto him that is athirst of the fountain of the water of life freely.

"He that overcometh shall inherit all things; and I will be his God, and he shall be my son."

The Book of Revelation, Chapter 21

Chapter Twenty

Julie heard the birds first. They had made their way to their bedrooms and, dreaming of wondrous and beautiful things, she had slept soundly in the arms of her husband.

But the birds caught her attention. Slowly she became aware of dusky outlines, dim but visible. The darkness was lifting. Tenderly she kissed Dave's lips and studied him with a new awareness. Recollections of all their past lives together flooded her mind and she felt the love they'd shared in each one. As soul mates, they'd sought each other in almost every lifetime. Then she saw an image of him fishing from a small boat in a beautiful mountain lake. He's having a dream, Julie thought, and I can share it. This new Dimension is going to be fun. He didn't stir so she gave him another kiss, pressing a little harder, and then another. She wondered if she had either lost her touch or he'd lost his senses.

One warm brown eye peeked up at her and the corner of his mouth twitched. "Don't stop now," he whispered.

"Ohhh, you! You were awake all the time!" she scolded, grinning.

"No, I just woke up—honest! Mmmm, what a wonderful way to wake up, my love. Are you okay? Did you sleep?"

"I did. And I'm … I feel glorious!" She truly felt she was overflowing with life. "The time of darkness is over. I can hear the birds singing and I'll bet the sun will be out soon. I can hardly believe it!"

"Uh-uh. Don't say that, babe."

"Don't say what? Oh, yes, I *can* believe it. I *know* the sun is coming up. I *know* it's the most exceptional day of our lives—all of our lives—over thousands and thousands of years." Julie wiggled out of his arms and lifted herself on one elbow.

"Hey, where do you think you're going?"

"There's so much to do. I need to get busy. Find some food, get those boards off the windows, take care of our family."

"No,"

"No?"

"No. Julie, we, all of us, have just made it through the Shift of the Ages, at least through the door, and we're in good hands. Everyone's still asleep and will wake up soon enough. Come on, babe. Relax, cuddle up, and just enjoy the moment. There isn't any hurry anymore. Let the peace roll over you. Let it in and make it your own. Okay?"

She looked into the tender eyes of her beloved, melted, and relaxed, really relaxed for the first time in a long, long time. Julie wasn't sure what had changed but she felt different, sounded different. And it *was* wondrous.

The Rocky Mountain cave dwellers were awakened once again by their loyal sentinel, Rusty, as he prowled around the perimeter, looking for an appropriate rock to mark, giving little woofs as if to say, "You know, I don't really want to do this in here but there's just not much choice!"

Jesse emerged from his dreams and, half awake, crawled out of his sleeping bag to the opening of the cave. He called Rusty to a rock at the entrance, safe enough for what needed to be done. It took a couple of minutes for Jesse to finally wake up. He was dimly aware that he had almost heard Rusty's thoughts. He shook his head as if to clear it and recalled the crazy events of the last night. When it dawned on him that he could actually see his dog once again, he let out a war hoop, bounded across the stone floor, and landed on top of his parents. "I can see! It's getting light! I can see again! We made it! Hey, come on, you guys! You gotta come look! Wake up, Dad! Mom! The trees are back!"

The disheveled group quickly untangled themselves and followed Jesse to the lip of the cave. A few lingering stars blinked in the dusky sky and faint outlines of pines, firs, and aspens were beginning to take shape. The trees had an unnatural glow around them, an aura. Birds sounded like a celestial choir, welcoming the beginning of a new day, a new life, a new world.

Megan and Steve stood in awe, their arms around each other and their children, overwhelmed at the sense of peace and contentment. Gazing at the slowly emerging vista in front of them, they wept tears of joy. There was no doubt their angels had been with them.

Mary awoke first. She lay still as her eyes adjusted and she realized the rooftop skyline was slowly materializing through the big picture window, the one that used to have blinds.

"Hallelujah!" she cried. "It's over! The worst is over and we're here. Oh, thank you, Lord."

A woolen blanket wrapped around her, she dropped to her knees in prayer. Emma, hearing her mother, uncurled her long legs, became aware that she could *see* her mother, and joined in.

Ellen and Chris, snuggled in each other's arms, slowly came out of their sleepy fog. Anxiety had disappeared. The feeling of being tossed about on a wave without a sandy shore was gone. In an extremely short time, they had graduated from spiritual grade school and arrived at a level that permitted them to cross into the Fifth Dimension. They quite simply just stared at the scene unfolding before their eyes; the last flickering star in the sky, the first glow of morning light, the dawn of a new day.

Chris had no idea what this day would bring, what the city would be like, what they should do. It didn't matter. This called for a celebration. There was *nothing* he and Ellen couldn't handle now.

Jon hit the floor with a thud. Stumbling over clothes and books, he yanked the temporary and inadequate window cover down and stared.

"It's happened! We've done it!" he yelled to the world. He gulped a deep breath of fresh air and shouted, *"Yes!"* punching the air with his fist for emphasis.

He couldn't wait any longer. He was ready to try translocating, a Fifth Dimension prediction that would make life a whole lot easier considering all the problems with the airlines. He looked down at his now-high water pants, and acknowledged a definite physical change. Rummaging around for some clothes that would fit, he finally sat down, yoga style, and began his focused breathing. In a state of deep bliss, he focused on his mother and brought her into his vision. Calling to her, he watched her sit up in bed and frown. He called again. She glanced around the room, puzzled. Then, centering his body, unblocking his mind, and with the words, "I am there," he consciously projected himself into the bedroom at Wind Dancer Ranch.

A hazy form began to materialize about ten feet from Julie and Dave, slowly taking shape as the sparkles united and a body formed. In a matter of seconds, there was little doubt who had joined them.

"Jon!" Julie shouted. "Oh my God, it's Jon! He's here! Jon, you're here!"

She leapt up and threw her arms around his neck. Lifting her in the air, he swung her around and leaned back, studying her face. It was still quite dark in the room but the planks on the windows allowed enough shafts of light through so they could see each other.

"Mom, you look absolutely stunning. You're getting young again." Then in an awed whisper, "I can't believe it. It's just like spirit told us it would be."

He swung her around again and she laughed, reveling in the joy of her son. Julie caught sight of herself in the full-length mirror and had to agree with Jon. She looked 20 years younger!

Everyone awakened with Julie's first yelp and came running. They stared, incredulous at the amazing reunion taking place before their eyes.

"What the heck is going on?" Bill asked. "Jon? Is that really you? How in blazes did you get here?"

"Damned straight, bro! Got here as soon as I could." Jon wrapped his brother in a big old bear hug, and then swept Joey up over his head amidst giggles and laughter.

"Hey, Joey! How's my boy? Bet you've got some stories to tell."

"Uncle Jon, you won't believe it. It was so dark and an angel came and it was just, it was just …" His words tumbled out faster than he could think of them.

"I bet it was, Joey. Tell me all about it later, okay?"

"Okay! I will!" But he hung onto his uncle's leg just in case Jon decided to evaporate.

Jon gave Kathy a hug, kissed the sleeping Erica on her forehead, then turned and shared a love-hug with Dave.

"Man, look at you! You look terrific! And that's a good thing if you're gonna be able to keep up with Mom," he laughed. "Where's Jeannie? She had her baby, didn't she." It wasn't a question.

He found them on Jeannie's makeshift bed in the living room, the baby snuggled in her arms. He smiled tenderly and his eyes filled with tears as he knelt beside them.

"How're ya doing, Momma Jean?" he asked.

"I'm okay, Jon. Sort of. I'm really worried about Jerry. He ran away. He's out there somewhere. But look—you have a new little niece." Her eyes glowed with love and pride as she introduced her daughter. "Her name is Angela."

Jon touched the newborn's hand, stroking it softly, provoking a smile on the rose bud lips. "Angela," he said. "What a great name. She's absolutely beautiful, Jeannie. What's this about Jerry? Where is he?"

"That's just it. I don't know where he is. He ran out of here when our baby was born, out into the cold and wind and darkness. He hasn't come back yet. I'm really scared, Jon."

"Why did he run out, for Pete's sake? What's going on?" Jon asked, looking at his mother.

Julie touched his arm. "Angela has spina bifida, Jon. It was too much for Jerry. I'm concerned that everything, the Photon energy and what's been happening, may have been more than he could handle."

Jon knew immediately what Julie was feeling, even thinking. "The Third Dimension. He wasn't ready to ascend into the Fifth. Jesus." He turned to Jeannie. "I promise you, little sister, we'll find him for you. We'll help him if we can. But it may take a while. We'll talk about it later but, in the meantime, you need to take care of yourself and your baby."

Joey squatted next to his cousin, patting her downy soft head. Very softly and without looking up, he whispered, "You're healed, Angela. It's okay. You're all better."

Bill knelt beside his son and put his arm around his shoulder. "Joey, she has a problem and it's not going to heal."

But Daddy, she is. It happened last night. Mister G told me. I just know she is," he insisted.

Bill didn't know whether to humor Joey or send him to "time out." It wasn't something he wanted to fool around with.

Julie was stunned. "Of course! I think he's right, Bill! Jeannie, unwrap Angela! Jon, help her!"

He folded the soft blanket back and Jean turned the baby onto her tummy. Angela's back was smooth and perfect, no hole, no scar. Jeannie gently rolled her onto her back on the mattress and Angela's legs began to kick and bend with vigor.

"Oh, my God! She *is* okay! She's *healed*!" Jeannie cried. "How did it happen? It's a miracle! How did it happen?"

"In the Fifth Dimension, all will be healed," Julie said softly. "Now I know it's true."

Everyone was speechless except Joey. He smiled with delight at his cousin, letting her grasp his finger as her dark blue eyes looked deeply into his. "You're okay now, Angela," he whispered. "God made you better. Some day I'll teach you how to ride a bike and milk a goat, okay?"

Bill was shocked. How had Joey known? What was it about Joey that made him different, doing and saying things that didn't seem normal? He'd been in denial that Joey possessed unusual talents but he couldn't ignore it any more. Bill squatted in front of Joey. "You've a lot to teach me, son."

"Okay, Dad." Joey looked a little bewildered. "You'll like Mister G. He used to be just kinda like a ghost but now he's real … at least to me."

Julie wiped the tears from her cheeks. "Okay, Jon, it's your turn. I don't see Tinker Bell and we know you're not Peter Pan, so tell us how you got here."

"You know we've just been waiting for it to manifest, Mom. You and I have kind of been practicing, communicating in a way that we could see each other in our mind's eye. We've come close to trans-locating before so this was a cinch. I don't know the whys and wherefores but when the Shift hit, a zillion changes took place. We're just not aware of them yet. It'll take a while to sink in. As you can see, or not see quite yet, there isn't any electricity. Just a little joke there. Sorry," he said with an apologetic smile.

He had everyone's attention, so he continued. "Batteries are shot so we'll be working with a new kind of energy, new fuels, stuff they probably used back on Atlantis. Our bodies have changed, inside and out. Our DNA has changed. But you won't really feel any different, except maybe healthier. I mean, look at you and Dave. You look like kids again," he smiled, exaggerating just a bit.

Jon took a deep breath. "You might not understand the words I'm using, but when we shifted into the Fifth, another veil was lifted, a big one. What's left is very thin now, the result being we all have telepathic abilities. In other words, no one gets away with fibs any more. If the thought is in your mind, everyone else will know what it is. It's probably gonna take a little time to develop fully before you get used to it. Who knows? It's all been speculation but now we get to find out if the prophets were right. Spooky, huh? It's sure as hell gonna make honest souls out of us in a hurry," he grinned.

Bill shook his head. "You're really stretching my belief system, Jon. Sure, you got here so there's got to be something weird going on. But I'm not telepathic."

"The first thing you'd better do, Bill, is to open your mind to possibilities. If you say you can't believe it, then you won't. The most powerful words in the universe are, 'It shall be given to you according to your beliefs.' The power is there for you to accept. Look at Angela. What an incredible example. If you believe it, you'll see it. As a matter of fact, it'd be a good idea for everyone to latch onto that real soon because there's a lot of manifesting to do to make our new world work." He looked at Joey. "Hey, buddy, send me a thought, okay?"

Joey closed his eyes, a smile tweaking the corners of his mouth.

Jon laughed. "No, Joey. Something I can share with the others."

"Okay, Uncle Jon. Here I go."

Jon paused a moment. "This is going to sound funny, but Joey is thinking about milking a goat. He's seeing himself squirting milk at a cat. Maybe I'm not getting it. Joey, is that what you were really thinking? If so, I've gotta ask why."

"Yup! Gram and I talked about it and she said she'd teach me how. So now I'm going to mani—what is it I'm gonna do?"

"You're going to manifest it. Make it happen." Jon looked at his mother and raised an eyebrow. "Good luck, Mom. I expect he'll be successful."

"Maybe you're telepathic, Jon, but I can't do that," Bill said.

"There's that lack of belief again. Come on, dude. Think positive. Allow it to happen. Relax and send a thought to someone and then confirm it. It might take some practice. In fact, I think it'll get real confusing because we may not be able to tell who is thinking what or even if it's our own thought. As things start flooding in, don't panic. Stay quiet, you know, like in meditation, and focus on who you want to communicate with. Make your own thoughts clear. It'll be okay. In fact, it'll be very enlightening."

Bill looked at Kathy. Why not? he thought. They were pretty much in tune anyway. Bill closed his eyes and visualized taking the moguls at Squaw Valley the way he used to.

Kathy smiled. "Skiing was your passion, Bill."

"Hey! It worked!" Bill was dumbfounded and Joey giggled. "Okay, Kathy," Bill said. "Now you think of something."

As Kathy thought of the last time they'd made love, Bill's mind filled with the images and he turned bright red, glad that they were in a darkened room.

"Whoa!" Jon said. "We all got that, and there are kids here!" In the laughter that followed, they felt the deep bond of souls who have incarnated together in every conceivable combination and love each other to the core of their beings.

Bill put his arm around his wife and gave her a gentle squeeze. The mutual tenderness had returned.

"Okay, you've got the gist of it," Jon said, "but there's much more. I 'thought' myself here and it probably doesn't take as much effort as I gave it. The first time you try something new, it's always a little scary. But this was easy. When you get your Fifth-Dimensional feet wet, you'll have a blast. Better stay here for a while, though. One step at a time. When the sun comes up, and it will, there'll be a new world to explore."

His excitement was catching, and after what they'd been through, it was a welcome relief. Julie sat cross-legged next to Jean and the baby, feeling as though she would burst with love for them all. She glowed and when her eyes met Dave's, the electricity was palpable.

She turned to Jon. "I haven't checked in on the rest of the family in ages. Lord! It seems like a lifetime! I feel sure they're okay but I'd like to find out. Do you think it's too soon?"

"They're gonna figure this all out for themselves before long, Mom. They'll probably end up here in Takoma Springs, but they may not realize it's possible yet. How about checking on them without going there? Maybe I'm selfish but I don't want you to disappear quite yet. Besides, you don't know where they are, do you?"

"Chris and Ellen are probably in their apartment but who knows where Steve and his family ended up. They're camping, and the last I 'saw' they were in a cave. They were safe, but the Rockies are vast."

"I'd like to know if they're all okay, too," Dave said. "Can you—would you—check on them, Julie?"

"I think you all could do it easily now but, yes, I will. In the meantime, maybe you guys would like some water, something to eat?"

"Food!" Jon said. "Right on! What have you got?"

"You can make food disappear faster than a vacuum cleaner," Julie laughed.

"I'll restrain myself. Besides I'll bet you have plenty. If not, we'll just manifest some more."

"Eat anything and everything you want, Jon. Your reputation precedes you. It was a joke, a stray thought."

Laughing, he gave Julie a hug. "I know, Ma." He turned to Jean. "I'll get you something, too, Jeannie. You must have worked up some appetite in the last few days. I want to hear the whole story."

"I'll join you, Jon," Dave said. "I think I know where things are. At least I used to. Then we'll get the boards off the windows, unless you think the wind is coming back."

"Who knows, but I doubt it. Nothing can ever blow again like it did this week."

Julie stood up and kissed Jean and her daughter on their respective foreheads and made her way to the meditation room.

Chapter Twenty-one

Steve was spellbound. The intense brilliance of the sunrise was like nothing he'd ever seen. The lush green pines and firs literally sparkled, standing out in relief against the multi-colored sky. If ever there was a definition of a deep blue crystal clear sky, this was it. He could almost make out the shapes of bands of shimmering light as they moved through space. The warmth felt so good, even Jesse and Mike were subdued by the wonder of it. This was going to be some kind of day. It would forevermore be "their cave," Steve thought. Whatever had happened to them had been profound.

"What did you say, Steve?" Megan asked.

"Nothing."

"I thought I heard you say something about the cave being ours forever."

"Well, yes. I mean, no. I didn't say it but I was thinking about that."

"But I heard you. I know I did," Megan said, trying to convince herself as well. "I just didn't catch it all."

"You must have read my thoughts."

"You're kidding. I can't do that."

"Mom said that these things could happen after the Shift. Well, we survived that. At least I don't think we've died and gone to the Promised Land. One of the gifts she mentioned was telepathy. How about sending me a thought? Let's try it."

"Okay." She was quiet for a moment. "Did you get it?"

"You're wondering how we're going to get off this cliff and find our way out of the woods again."

"Yes! That's exactly what I was thinking about!" Megan said surprised. She wasn't really sure she wanted him to know all of her thoughts.

"Hey, this could be fun," Steve grinned. "Jesse, what are you thinking?"

"I'm hungry!"

"I *know* that! I meant, think something so I can guess it."

Jesse closed his eyes.

"Okay, you're still hungry, right?"

"You got it, Dad. Starved!"

"So much for creativity. Mikey, I'm tuning into you. Oh. You need to go to the bathroom. Let's take care of that right now."

"How did you know that, Daddy? Can you tell just by looking at me?" He had an alarmed look on his face.

Steve laughed. "No, tiger, it doesn't show on the outside. It's a mental thing called telepathy. We've got a lot of new stuff to explore and try out, guys. It's like getting new computer games but this time there aren't any manuals. This new world is pretty exciting. Funny, I keep getting the feeling that Mom is around. I almost feel like she can hear me. Do you feel it, Megan?"

Megan closed her eyes for a moment. "Yes, I do! I bet she's thinking about us and we're catching her thoughts. Hey, Julie! We can feel you! Are you thinking of us?" she said, laughing at her own silly notion.

Steve and Megan looked at each other in stunned disbelief when they distinctly heard Julie say, "Yes!"

Dave tiptoed into the meditation room. He didn't like leaving Julie alone. He was afraid she might up and disappear. He wasn't ready for that yet.

When Julie opened her eyes, they were brimming with tears, her radiant face bathed in the soft, gentle candlelight. Dave marveled at the beauty of this woman, his wife, as he often did.

"You don't look too bad yourself," she said, laughing. "You've lost that spare tire and you're standing much taller. In fact, you'd better sit down before I have my way with you."

Dave made himself comfortable.

"They're safe, Dave. Steve and Megan and the kids appear to be okay. I saw them in their cave. They just realized they could read each other's minds. It was like watching them open Christmas presents. They even felt my presence and responded back to me. I can't wait to visit them." Seeing Dave's frown, she quickly added, "Don't worry, honey, I won't go yet."

"Good! Do you think you could tune into Chris and Ellen now? Just to make sure they're okay."

"Of course. Let's do it together. You can do it, too, you know. Come on. Sit down by me. I'll guide you into a centered place, visualize them and see what happens."

"Are you sure I can do this?"

"Of course. You always could. We used to tune into each other, remember? Same thing. Let's give it a try."

He made himself comfortable. White candles glowed in the dim room and the scent of incense tickled his nose. Crystals sparkled in the flickering candlelight. The ambiance was spiritual, safe and nurturing.

They closed their eyes and Julie led him through a deepening of awareness, surrounding and protecting them both in the white light of God. He drifted down as he relaxed and released the world from his thoughts, from his body. Floating in space, he felt lightheaded and free. Although he'd meditated before, this was a new experience. Julie's voice sounded far away, as though in an echo chamber.

"And now," Julie continued, "using your third eye, open your vision to Chris. Bring him into your thoughts. Ask mentally for his spirit to be shown to you. Do this with deep love and know that God is protecting you and him during this process. Let this happen now."

Dave felt like a shooting star. He didn't have wings, but he shot through space at an incredible speed. He wasn't afraid; he observed and experienced everything at the same time. Then he heard a voice in the distance.

"Dad! Oh, my God, Ellen, it's Dad!"

Dave felt a little dizzy and wondered where he was.

"Dad! It's me, Chris. Is that really you?"

Dave felt his son's arms encircle his body, wrapping him in the most incredible sense of love he could ever have imagined. His eyes began to focus and he grabbed Chris in a hug that made him cough.

Chris laughed. "Hey, not so hard, Dad. How did you get here? You just appeared, for God's sake! No one was here and then you were standing there. Like in *Star Trek.* I can't believe it! How did you do it?" Chris was totally blown away.

Dave, grinning from ear to ear, found his balance and turned to Ellen. She threw her arms around him. "Hey, it's okay, El. You made it through. Please don't cry. Everything's okay."

"I can't help it. I'm just so happy to see you!" She pulled herself together. "It was so strange. Chris was wonderful and Mary and Emma were fantastic. I don't know what would have happened if it weren't for them. I have no idea how you got here, Dave, but don't you dare leave us."

"I'm not even sure myself," Dave said, grinning broadly. "Julie and I were going to 'tune in' as she calls it, to make sure you were safe. She does it a lot and, with the Shift, she said we could all do it. I expected to see you in my head, like a movie. But all of a sudden I was here. Just like that," he added, snapping his fingers.

"That's awesome," Chris said, trying to absorb the possibilities.

"Jon did it, too, but he did it on purpose. He was in San Francisco and he just appeared in our bedroom. It was an amazing thing. I guess I did whatever he did. This is great. I just hope I can get home again. July will go nuts when she sees I'm not there."

"Well, don't go yet," said Chris, grabbing his father's arm.

"I'm not going anywhere until I know everything that's been happening to you. And, by the way, you've got an absolutely beautiful little niece. Jean had the baby yesterday."

"You're kidding! Ellen, did you hear that? Jeannie had her baby. I'm an uncle and that means you're an aunt. Uncle Chris," he said, trying the new title on for size. "Is she okay? I mean, what a hell of a time to give birth! What's her name? And how's Jerry doing?"

"Slow down, Chris. One question at a time. She's great. They both are. Her name is Angela. I think because an angel helped deliver her. Then an incredible miracle happened." He paused. "I'm not sure about Jerry."

Ellen raised her eyebrows. "An *angel* delivered the baby? A miracle? What are you talking about, Dave?"

"It's a long story. Very long. I'll tell you all about it in a minute, but tell me about you guys first."

"Well," Chris began as they settled on the couch, "it all started a few days ago with the riots and … jeez, Dad, I want you to meet two of the most incredible ladies I've ever known." Chris jumped up and looked around the room. "Ellen, where did they go?"

"I don't know. They were right here. When Dave popped in, I forgot all about them. Oh dear!" She ran down the hall. "Mary! Emma! Where are you?" Silence filled the apartment. "Chris, they're gone! They're not here!"

"The dead bolt is still in place," said Chris. "No one left that way. Do you think they might have …? Could they have done what you did, Dad? Maybe they went to check on their own family."

"If I can do it, anybody can. Who are they? What were they doing here?"

"Well, that's a long story, too," Chris said. "I just hope they're okay. I want to be able to see them again. I feel like we know them in a very special way."

"You'll see them again if you want to," Dave said. "In fact, I think it's almost too easy now. If you let your thoughts focus on another planet, you'd probably have the chance to explore it. We've got so much to be thankful for. I feel so fantastic and I don't know how to describe it all—what happened, how I feel—"

Chris stared at his father, a puzzled look on his face. "You know, Dad, you do look different. You've dropped some years. I mean, it's not that you looked old before, but you've changed. Have you lost weight, changed the color of your hair?"

"Wait 'till you see Julie," Dave said proudly. "I've learned a whole lot about a lot of things lately. I'd have never made it home from L.A. if God hadn't been watching over me. Nor would Bill. Or any of the others for that matter. Our angels were on double duty. Maybe your friends were angels, too. Maybe they were here to help you through the Shift. Who knows? But one thing I know for sure: Prayers are important. Whether you're needing help or giving thanks for the help you got, prayers are always heard."

"You know, I was always kind of embarrassed just saying the word 'pray.' Pretty stupid of me," admitted Chris. "So it's really new for us. But I have the feeling it's going to be a major part of our lives from now on."

Ellen nodded. She had a lot to pray about. She placed her fingers gently on her upper right breast to touch the unwanted lump that constantly occupied her thoughts and emotions. With a puzzled look on her face, she quickly moved her hand in all directions. "Chris, I can't feel it … it's not there! Something's happened!"

"What? Are you serious? Are you sure, honey?"

"Yes! See if you can … I mean, it's just not there anymore!"

Dave cleared his throat. "May I ask what's gone?" It was perfectly obvious it wasn't the breast that was missing.

"Ellen found a lump on her breast a couple of weeks ago. I was going to take her to the hospital next week. But it looks like a miracle has happened."

"Healing miracles are happening everywhere right now," Dave said, hugging both of them. "And if you think that's amazing, wait until I tell you about Angela!"

Chapter Twenty-two

It had indeed taken Julie by surprise. As she tuned into Chris, her head began spinning. Quickly grounding herself, her vision cleared and to her amazement, she saw Dave embracing Chris. Her heart began to pound like a jackhammer. Then she relaxed as she realized what had happened. It was a good thing Jon had successfully ventured through the universe first so she knew it could be done. Of course, it might have been better if she'd helped Dave ground himself, but she'd taken it for granted that he'd do that. She noticed a woman and a teenager in the room, the ones she'd seen before, radiating the most beautiful, shimmering light. As she watched, they joined hands, smiled at each other, and simply disappeared.

The kids appeared overjoyed to see Dave. She gently withdrew her energy from the apartment in North Carolina, bringing the connecting cords back into her own auric field.

In her meditative state, Julie let her thoughts travel to her friend, Rachel, wondering how she had fared. With all that had transpired, she needed to connect with her old soul mate. No sooner had she let the desire manifest than she felt a jolt, a sort of mid-air collision.

"Rachel!"

"Julie!"

They hugged each other hard, laughing and dancing around. "Where are we?" asked Julie.

"I haven't a clue. I just thought of you and wham! You were here."

"I don't know what's going on but for the sake of my sanity," Julie said, "would you please join me in thinking ourselves into your house or mine?"

"Good idea, love. Let's go to yours."

"Wonderful. Here we go."

"That was really bizarre," Julie said, back in her meditation room. "But you're here. I can touch you. Just like Jon."

"Did Jon do this, too?"

"Sure did. Surprised the heck out of us. And Dave did it by accident to Chris and Ellen's place. He's there now. So tell me. What's happened for you? How's the family? Is everyone all right? You look stunning—your skin, your figure, everything about you. You're a new you, Rachel."

"Thanks. The same goes to you. I bet Dave's in seventh heaven," she said with a wink.

They settled themselves in Julie's special room, taking turns spinning stories of the adventure, sharing the laughter and the tears. One of the special gifts of the Fifth Dimension was the ability to know all one's past lives, to be aware of those lifetimes. Rachel and Julie had been together many, many times in different relationships, always supportive as family or friends.

"Do you remember the lifetime we spent as nuns in the convent in Europe?" Julie giggled. "We sure loosened up that group!"

Rachel laughed until her sides hurt. "Let's go back further. We were sisters, I think. In Atlantis."

"And Dave was our father!" Julie said. "He's been watching out for me for a long time." She paused. "Oh, Rachel, we were buddies in a war of some kind. I can feel the pain, and you saved my life. There's so much to learn, isn't there?"

Rachel's family had been anxious throughout the Shift but they had made it through. "Now they're like sponges, absorbing whatever I can give them. I'm concerned about Robert and his family. I've tried to tune in but haven't connected. Do you think I could find them in the Third if they didn't make the Shift?"

"I have to believe that. And if I get there, I'll look for them."

"Thanks, Julie. And now I'd better get back. But I'll see you soon!"

The brilliance of the new day peeked through cracks in the plywood window covers and they all, even little Angela, moved out to the deck to soak up the warmth, the light, the incredible fresh air, the intense luminescence spread before them.

Max ran for a post, then a tree, re-marking his territory. Sandy stretched languidly in the warmth of the sun. The trees were brilliant, radiating shimmering colors out into the atmosphere. Fields glowed in shades of gold and green, and the rich brown earth had a palpable softness just asking to be held and sifted through loving hands. A soft warm breeze whispered through the trees, ruffling the hay in the fields and caressing their faces. A family of elk grazed in the field and lifted their heads. They, too, had beautiful auras.

"Dear God, I've never seen *anything* like this!" Julie said in wonderment. "I feel as if I'm in a painting, a make-believe place."

"Everything is so beautiful," Kathy said almost reverently. "The colors are so deep and pure." Feeling euphoric, she took Erica and Joey's hands and descended the steps, heading for the open field.

As all three hunched over a small treasure that had caught Joey's eye, Julie vividly recalled going through the same motions with her own young charges, sharing the excitement of discovering a small flower, a tiny bug, or even a pretty stone.

Jon put his arm around her shoulders as the two of them walked toward the grazing elk. "Those were wonderful times, weren't they, Mom? You used to get excited with us and always had a story for whatever we found. You made the sun shine and gave meaning to the world, even back then. You gave me my life, then filled it with wonder and love and support." He looked out over the panoramic vista. "And you're still doing it, Mom. I guess it goes on forever. I understand now why we've shared so many lives together as mother and son."

The bull elk was majestic with an enormous rack, and the gentle cow with her soft brown eyes stood quietly beside him, their young happily nibbling the tall grass as Jon and Julie approached. Awe spread across Julie's face as she realized she was aware of the elks' thoughts. "Jon, are you 'hearing' them, too? It's amazing. They're sending us such love."

"Yeah. They know they're safe now. We can talk to them, too," he said, gently stroking the neck of the huge bull.

"Welcome to the new world, you magnificent creatures. You have a beautiful family," Julie said. As the elk seemed to nod in agreement, Julie shook hers in wonderment.

Jon squeezed her shoulders and kissed the top of her head as they started back to the house. Julie thought her heart would burst. Hearing Jon's words and feeling his emotions at the same time, knowing the depths of his feelings beyond the words, was a new sensation. The openness shattered barriers and tumbled walls. She looked at her son. "I love you so very much, Jon. You'll never know how much."

His eyes glowed brightly as he looked into her soul. "Yes, I do. I love you, too, Mom."

Bill and Dave tore the plywood off the windows and the house was once again bathed in sunshine. The magnificent view, including the now-dazzling Crystal Peak, was breathtaking. Julie had always known the mountain generated high energy but now she saw its rainbow aura reaching miles above it. What more could we ask, she thought, except to know where Jerry is and if he's all right. Deep in her heart, she knew he was trapped in the Third Dimension.

With a sigh, she turned to Jon. "I need to feed the animals. It's been way too long."

"Want some company?"

"No, thanks. I think I need to be alone for a little while. Overload, you know. Maybe you could help the guys."

They shared a special smile.

Julie pulled on her work boots and headed down the well-worn path. She threw open the barn doors, letting the light stream in, and was greeted by assorted neighs, bleats, and cackles. The cats came running, meowing and rubbing their soft bodies around her legs. She greeted them all, opened the paddock doors to the wild delight of the horses, filled the water buckets, fed the goats, cats, and chickens, and found several fresh eggs for breakfast.

After cleaning the stalls and laying down fresh hay for their beds, she washed her hands and headed for Daisy Mae and her distended udder. Milk pail in hand, Julie carefully squatted on the small wooden stool and began rhythmically squeezing and pulling, telling her what a wonderful, giving goat she was. A tap on her shoulder made her jump.

"Joey! I didn't hear you come in."

"I know. I wanted to surprise you—and I did! Grammy, you promised I could try milking and squirting a cat. Can I, please? Can I?"

"Tell you what, Joey. You find the cat while I give Daisy Mae a little relief. Then you can give it a try. We'll see if we can do what Uncle Clarence used to do. Okay?"

He was off scouting the barn in an instant, his eyes glowing with excitement. It didn't take long to uncover a reluctant feline. Grasping the big cat around the middle, he carried his prize to Julie, with the cat's tail flicking angrily. Telling his prize to sit still, he set her down, but she disappeared quicker than a bolt of lightning.

"Hey! Come back here!" he yelled, running after her.

Julie laughed. He would have to call on some power besides physical to accomplish this task.

Head hanging low, Joey shuffled back to Julie. "I must have done something wrong, Gram." Dejected, he plunked himself on a bale of hay and rested his determined chin on his fists. Being rejected by a cat had hurt his ego. "There's another way to do it, isn't there?"

"Cats don't like to be manhandled, but if you try to talk to them with your mind, it might help. Then again, the angels might lend a helping hand. I think you can accomplish anything you want to now. Why don't you give it a try?"

He jumped off the hay and coiled himself, yoga style, next to Julie. He touched thumbs and middle fingers together, rested them on his knees, and closed his eyes. Where he went, Julie didn't know, but she honored the silence and waited. It didn't take long. Not one but two barn cats came around the corner and cautiously made their way towards Joey. They sat six feet away, their tails curled around their feet.

"Joey, look," she whispered.

He opened his eyes and a triumphant smile spread across his face.

Julie put a finger to her lips, gesturing for him to come closer. She gently placed his hands on Daisy's teats and covered them with her own. She squeezed and pulled but not much happened, certainly not enough to create a six-foot stream.

Joey looked at her questioningly. They tried again. Julie couldn't get the grip right with his hands there.

She couldn't explain what happened next. A being joined them and although she couldn't see him, she knew without a doubt that her uncle was there. Slowly Julie released her hands from Joey's and as she did, Joey began squeezing and pulling, gently but firmly, and a steady stream of milk hit the bucket. She watched as Joey turned his hand to the side, aimed for a cat, and pulled the teat. A stream of rich goat's milk shot through the air and landed on the cat's face. A second yank covered the other cat's nose and whiskers. Julie wished she'd had a camera.

Awe at his own achievement rendered Joey speechless. He looked at Julie, then at the cats, then at his hands. His lips formed a smile, his eyes twinkled, and Julie heard him say, "Thank you." He released his hands from the goat and once again Julie took over.

Joey let out a belly laugh. "Look, Grammy! Look at the cats!"

Pink tongues were stretched to the limit, licking the sweet milk from dripping whiskers. Their eyes crossed as they tried to see what was covering their noses. Julie and Joey's laughter echoed throughout the barn. Joey ran off with a story to tell to whoever would listen.

"Congratulations, Julie. That was beautiful."

Puzzled, Julie glanced around the barn. "Who said that? Who spoke to me?"

Misty neighed from her stall and Julie knew. "Thank you, old girl," she said, stroking the horse's sleek neck. "I'm going to like communicating with you like this."

Misty tossed her head with understanding.

Unseen forces had surely protected the greenhouse. Kathy and Erica joined Julie for the rounds, touching, talking to, and admiring the rich growth of her garden. Julie was sure it hadn't looked this good a few days ago. The plants glowed with soft pastel auras and stood straighter and stronger as Julie sent them love. It reminded her of Findhorn where everything was as lush as they believed it to be.

"You know, Kathy, some of the phrases we grew up with are so disgustingly limited. Things like 'I just can't believe it.' No wonder negative thoughts get implanted in our cells and then we never know why things don't happen. Or if they do, it's not what we really wanted. I truly believe those days are gone forever."

Inhaling a final deep breath of the rich greenhouse aroma, they headed back to the deck. Julie wanted Dave to return home. There were practical things to be taken care of that only he could handle. Besides, she missed him. The thought didn't take long to manifest in North Carolina.

"Uh-oh," Dave said. "Julie wants me back home. It's time for me to go. I'll see you guys later."

Chris promised they'd try transporting themselves to Wind Dancer Ranch in the near future, adding they'd better stay grounded for a while, at least until they got their space legs.

Unsure of whether it would work, Dave closed his eyes, visualized Julie and his home in his third eye, and whispered, "I am there." And he was.

Chapter Twenty-three

Julie began to explore the Shift changes. Every moment was a delight and all the tomorrows promised more mind-bending adventures and challenges in the Fifth Dimension. She had to admit she was going to miss flipping a light switch, at least until something better came along. Fossil fuels were done, finished. Cars, what was left of them, were permanently parked—at least for a while. Hopefully bicycles hadn't lost any important parts.

If some people weren't ready to trans-locate, horses could be used for transportation until new fuels were available. Alternative fuels had been developed besides solar; they just weren't in use yet, thanks to unending lobbying in the government. Interesting thought. Would there even be a government now? She had no idea.

Special beings had been planted on Earth to develop new environmentally friendly materials but countries had not been interested, especially the United States. Americans had had it too good; there hadn't been any motivation to look for alternatives. Politics kept less expensive, innovative methods from disrupting large corporations. But the previous year had brought forth more soul-searching and research, creating more open minds than ever before. Cataclysmic earth changes tend to do that but it was too little too late.

She wondered what was happening downtown, in the next state, in other countries, in other worlds. How many had survived? What about those she knew personally? Had they given in to fear? Had they been in the wrong place at the wrong time? People would always be where they needed to be, no matter what the consequences. She wanted to check on friends and neighbors but she wasn't ready to go there yet.

One thing was for sure: She needed new clothes. It was time to improvise. Cottons, woolens and other natural fibers were in, polyesters out. Soft cotton diapers were in, disposables out, gone, disintegrated forever. Laundry would be a challenge until the water pump worked again.

Julie wandered around the deck lost in thought, and found herself by her favorite niche where she had tuned into her loved ones a lifetime ago. Had it been only a matter of days? Making herself comfortable in her quiet retreat, she contemplated the changes she had seen in her family, physical as well as mental, emotional, and spiritual. They were growing in so many ways. The children were fascinating to watch, especially Joey, who was growing up moment by moment. There was something new in his eyes. He was a wise soul, possibly even a Master. Erica was too young to analyze yet but her energy level and curiosity had intensified immediately after the Shift. And there must be something special about Angela, who chose to be born at the Shift of the Ages. Mike and Jesse were twins but so different. She was sure they had special roles to live out during this time in earth's history. She missed them.

Julie focused on Steve and his family but pulled herself back, not wanting to accidentally translocate to a cave just yet. Maybe

Dave or Jon would join her soon on a space excursion, a vacation in the Rockies.

The warmth of the sun dispelled the cold dampness inside the cave, transforming it into a completely different domain. It was amazing what a little sunshine could do. Taking stock of their supply of dried food and water, Steve decided now might be the time to head for home. He didn't look forward to the treacherous descent.

"Okay, gang," he announced, "this is it. Here's the plan: We're going to head home."

"Yea! When can we leave? Now, Dad? Can we leave now?" Mike asked.

"Oh boy, home!" Jesse said. "But how're we gonna get down?"

"Very carefully, right, Steve?" Megan had had enough camping to last a lifetime.

"Yes, carefully. With the ropes we've got, we should be able to lower Rusty in a makeshift sling. It will be safer than the way we got him up here," he said, remembering his experience all too well. "So let's pack up and see what we can do."

Mike rode on Steve's back first. The foot and handholds were locked in Steve's memory, so the descent was smooth and safe. He felt lighter and so did his son. Breathing a sigh of relief, he headed back up the cliff.

They shackled Rusty, wrapped him securely in a makeshift arrangement, and slowly lowered him over the side. He was rather unhappy about it but at least he wasn't barking in Steve's ear.

An indignant howl that sounded like the call of the wild echoed through the valley as Rusty swayed on the harness. Mike caught him and released the restraints. Free at last, he ran in circles watering every tree and bush he could find.

The backpacks were lowered, and with a final good-bye to their cave, Steve climbed down with Jesse on his back and Megan followed.

It was an arduous and scary descent for Megan. Her knees were weak and fingers bleeding by the time she reached bottom and fell into Steve's welcoming arms. She began searching for the bandages, then noticed that her fingers were fine—no cuts, no scratches. That was strange, she thought. They'd been bloody a few minutes ago and now they were fine. She shrugged, tied a string around her ponytail, and hoisted her backpack over her shoulders. They still had a long way to go.

Nothing looked the same. Trees and bushes had metamorphosed. They were magnificent and brilliant. Rocks and stones glistened and the sky was an intense shade of blue. It was indeed a new beginning.

Eventually they found the trail and followed it down the mountainside. The remainder of their food quickly disappeared when they stopped to eat. Rusty found a cold mountain stream and slurped his fill with gusto. They all drank. Steve refilled their canteens.

He had an eerie feeling of being watched, a strange but not frightening sensation. He couldn't see anything and Rusty wasn't disturbed. Perhaps they were angels or elementals—elves, fairies—beings who watched over the land. Why not, Steve thought. Better that than a bear or hungry mountain lion! He'd never seen either on his hikes but footprints proved they shared the same mountain trails.

"I see it, I see it! There's the Explorer!" Megan cried.

The boys raced ahead, shouting their exuberance. Rusty was excited, too, and ran in circles around his buddies nearly tripping them up. Their car had suffered a few scratches from falling branches but no serious damage had been done. Steve opened the back and stashed the gear and dog inside. They all got in and settled down. Steve turned the key. Nothing. He turned it again. Still nothing. He tried again, to no avail.

"What is it, Steve? What's wrong?" Megan asked.

"I dunno," he said. "Maybe it's got something to do with all the other stuff going on. Boy, I wish I'd paid more attention to the information my folks sent. Do you remember Mom saying anything about cars not running?"

"You kept her from talking to me about that nonsense, but it *wasn't* nonsense; we just thought it was."

"What's up, Dad?" Mike asked. "Why aren't we leaving?"

"There's something wrong with the car. It won't start and I've got to figure out why." He got out and began tinkering under the hood. Everyone followed.

"Dad?"

"Not now, Jess."

"But, Dad," Jesse persisted.

"Don't whine, Jess. What did I just say? Let me concentrate on this, okay?" Steve was more than a little stressed. Mechanical things had never been his forte.

"Take it easy, honey," Megan said. "We'll get it going. There's no hurry. We've made it this far."

Steve walked around the vehicle as though looking for a sign.

Megan looked at Jesse. "What is it? Do you need to go to the bathroom?"

"No, I just went, Mom," he said, rolling his eyes. "I wanted to tell Dad about something I remembered Gram saying, something about cars not running because of the gas, and that batteries wouldn't work either."

"Steve! Where are you?"

"Under here! Under the car!"

She got down on her hands and knees and found Steve lying there looking at Lord-knows-what because Steve sure didn't know.

"Jesse may have the answer to why the car won't start."

"What are you talking about?"

"Ask him. And if he's right, I have no idea what we're going to do. Are you going to come out of there or not?"

"I'll talk to Jesse," he said, wriggling out from under the Explorer.

The pieces began to fit. Jesse got a hug and an apology for his efforts.

"Family conference time," Steve said. "We've got to regroup. I know where we are but I don't know how far it is to find help. Or if anyone could even help us if we find them. Any suggestions?"

"You and me could go for help, Dad," Mike said.

"You and I," Megan corrected. "And I don't want to stay here alone with Jesse. If you don't come back for a long time, what would we do?"

"I think we should stick together," Jesse said.

"Any particular reason?" Steve asked.

"We've done pretty good so far, being a team," Jesse said. "Even Rusty. We can't stay here so we should all start hiking. Maybe we can find some food or something and walk all the way home if we have to."

Nothing ventured, nothing gained, thought Steve. “Okay, let’s do it. Let’s pack up, lock the car and become pioneers. This’ll be another family adventure, just like in the movies. Right, boys?” He expressed more bravado than he felt.

“Right, Dad!” they said in unison.

The hours sped by and their stomachs churned for nourishment. They found a sheltered area under some trees near a stream and pitched their tent. A crackling fire took the chill and dark shadows away and hot cups of Indian tea warmed their bellies.

It was going to be a long night.

Chapter Twenty-four

Julie and I are going to call it a night," Dave said. "We haven't had much sleep lately."

Julie took his hand and gave him a knowing smile. "If there's anything you guys need, tell me now. We should all be set for the night. Tomorrow promises to be another adventure, if the predictions are true. So sleep well, my loves. Good night and God bless. I love you."

"Hey, Mom, wait a minute," Bill said. "What's going to happen tomorrow? You can't just leave and not tell us."

"Watch me," Julie laughed. "Seriously, Bill, who really knows what will take place? I sure don't. Maybe nothing. Just open your minds to the unusual, the unbelievable, the inconceivable. That should about cover it."

Dave guided Julie to their room by candlelight. She felt strangely shy. There was little doubt what Dave had in mind, but there was something much deeper happening, something on a level she hadn't experienced before.

Closing the door, Dave turned to the woman he loved with all his heart. She was radiantly beautiful, her lips soft and welcoming. Brushing the hair from her forehead, he gently kissed her.

Undressing each other, they caressed and admired each other's body. He picked her up and lay her down on the soft quilt. Neither had ever felt such intense passion. Their bodies joined and quickly soared to a rapturous climax.

In awe of the emotions that had burned in their hearts, bodies, and souls, they basked in the afterglow of the deepest love and commitment they had ever known. Whispering words of love, they promised to be together forever and ever, and knew it to be true.

Something beyond their comprehension had been liberated between them. Recognition of their past was revealed. The culmination of hundreds of lifetimes as lovers, never able to join together as man and wife, lifetimes of longing from afar, had kept them apart over and over again. Their souls had chosen this momentous period, the time of the Shift, to incarnate together once more to live out their twin flame connection as man and wife. They would never again be separated by any force in the universe. Reunited at last, they were finally complete, one with each other and with God.

It was a fitting close to an incredible day, a day of revelation, self-empowerment, deepening spiritual beliefs, and a great deal of love. They'd been truly blessed.

Julie slipped out of bed at first light, quickly dressed, put on her work boots, snuggled into a warm jacket, and headed for the barn. The sun shining on the mountain range created a glowing aura on the horizon. A few clouds of violet, pink, yellow, and orange shimmered against the cerulean sky. The air was crisp and pure, the world silent except for early birds chirping and singing for the sheer joy of it. Julie hugged herself and twirled in a circle, smiling at the night before.

Singing softly, she watched Max and Sandy explore enticing scents and mark their territory again. That was a never-ending project. She opened the barn doors wide, letting fresh air and sunshine fill the building. The horses picked up her telepathic image of the pasture and trotted out into the sunshine, bucking and snorting playfully.

She petted the cats, collected the eggs and headed for the door. Gasping, she nearly dropped her basket. A man stood silhouetted in the doorway. The sun was behind him so she couldn't see his face but the glow encompassed him in a halo.

"Oh! You startled me. I didn't hear anyone coming up the driveway. I'm Julie. May I help you?"

"Hello, Julie," he said quietly. He stepped inside, a beautiful smile radiating across his face.

"Oh my God! Dad!" she gasped. "It's really you!" The eggs dropped to the floor as she flung her arms around his neck. "You're here! I can touch you! I can see you!" Tears flowed as she held him tightly. His strong reassuring arms hugged her close.

"I love you, sweetheart."

"Oh, Dad, I love you, too. I've missed you so much."

"I've been here, you know, communicating with you often."

"I know and that's been wonderful, but it's not the same as seeing you in person. How did you do it? I mean, you're here in body and flesh. You've come back from the dead," she said in wonderment.

He laughed. "No, my dear Julie. I was never dead. You know that. You helped me understand that after your mother passed on. My body withered away, but I—me, the soul that I am—have been here all along. You didn't understand that in the Third

Dimension, the so-called real world filled with hate and crime and judgment. Your spiritual awakening allowed you to slowly transition into the Fourth, and now the Shift has catapulted you and others into the Fifth level. We're meeting, you and I, on a middle ground of energy. Your vibrations have been raised, I've lowered mine, and here we are." He smiled. "It's only the beginning."

"Why? What else is there, Dad? Is there something more I should know?"

"You know it already on some level, but I wanted to prepare you so you can share this knowing with your family, our family. The things taking place will shake them up a bit. You and I communicated for years through thoughts or table-tipping. That won't be necessary anymore. Just as you've all achieved mental telepathy, there are many other gifts you now have that will, using your words, blow your mind. Strange phrase. Nevertheless, playing with these gifts will be like a game. What I want you to understand now is that all your loved ones, your grandparents, your ancestors, can and will be appearing to you when it's the right time. You will know them because you've known them before, in other lives. The lives you've lived before will be, are now being, integrated into you as one being. The knowledge you've attained through lifetimes will easily be at your disposal."

So that's what happened last night, Julie thought.

"What was that, Julie?"

Blushing, she said, "Nothing, Dad. Just something personal."

He laughed. "Okay, I won't trespass there. We do have our ethics in this new dimension."

"What else is happening, Dad?" Julie wanted all the information she could get. "When will I be able to see Mom again?"

"Whenever you're ready. I'm acting as sort of your Town Crier, announcing coming events, issuing warnings of change—wonderful change, I might add. You're becoming aware of the past relationships you've had with people who are in your life now. You'll know, for instance, really *know*, when you and your children first incarnated together, the intertwined connections you've experienced of learning and growing and supporting each other from the beginning of life itself.

"You first incarnated in a group of three hundred on another planet and, for the most part, the same souls have chosen to reincarnate together through many thousands of lifetimes. The awareness of the relationships, the contracts you made with each other, will be revealed to you, all of you, beginning today. You'll probably only be given what you can handle and accept, more for you than for the others. There will be surprises and understanding. Issues and conflicts will be understood, forgiven, and love will supersede all other emotions."

"I feel humbled, Dad, and so grateful to be able to experience this."

"You're ready. Through lifetimes, you've prepared for this. And you're here now to help others through these changes. Nothing, absolutely nothing, will be impossible for you to accomplish. But you'll need to acknowledge this inside yourself before you can manifest it." He paused. "There's one other thing I want to share with you this morning."

She wasn't sure she wanted to hear any more. Certainly this was enough for any one person to absorb at one time.

"I understand that you've already had to absorb a lot of information," he said, reading her mind, "but awareness is very important. You've been preaching that to your family and friends for a long time now. You told them to be aware that there were changes coming but they only half believed you. Change is frightening for some. I just want you to be aware, Julie."

She nodded, not sure what to expect next.

"On Earth, today and forever more, there are beings of great light, Masters from the highest realms in the universe walking amongst you. You will know them. You have communicated with several, using your tools. Know that the Archangels are here, your special friends and guides who have been leading you and teaching you. Gandhi and Buddha are here. So is Jesus of Nazareth. They may not look as you would expect, but nevertheless you will know them. Mother Mary and many others are back to help with the transition, to help you help those who linger in the Third and Fourth Dimensions, unable to take the leap of faith. These beings will manifest wherever they're needed."

Julie was skeptical. "This is a stretch for me, Dad. Where are they? In Denver? London? Takoma Springs? It's so hard to comprehend."

"I know. The knowledge will come when you're ready to receive it. Trust, Julie. Trust in God and trust in yourself. I might as well tell you that you will also encounter beings from other realms. Extraterrestrials. ETs. They might not look human. They may have different shapes, colors or sizes. They may appear as some sort of animal, but their intelligence is no less or more than yours. Don't ever forget, we are all One. Be open to what they can teach you for they have much to share. Accept them and love them as your own family. The love will return tenfold."

Julie simply stood there, her eyes slightly glazed.

"Are you all right, my child? Have I shared too much? You are a Master yourself, you know. The knowledge is buried at the moment. But you've been a guide and leader for so many through the past few years, I felt you needed to stay on top of it, so to speak. Forgive me if I've assumed too much."

Julie shook her head as if to clear away cobwebs. "Yes. I mean no. You haven't assumed too much; and yes, I'm all right. I'm just overwhelmed. I appreciate what you've done and said. You're right. As things come up, I hope I'll be able to explain and alleviate any fears. There's so much information to assimilate, though." She was definitely over-enlightened.

"It's time for me to go, Julie. You have company heading your way. I'll be with you, but not visible to others yet. When it's time, we'll have a reunion to end all reunions. Maybe some Maine lobsters, topped off with steamed clams and corn on the cob." He smiled that wonderful smile that crinkled the corners of his eyes. He hugged her and faded into nothingness.

"Bye, Dad," Julie said. "See you soon."

"Gramma! Gramma!" Joey called, running into the barn. "Come quick! Grandpa's been looking for you! You gotta come right away!"

"What's the matter?"

"I dunno. He just said, 'Go find your grandmother and tell her I need her.' So I did."

"Hold on a sec, Joey."

Julie stopped, closed her eyes and focused on her husband, meeting his thoughts at the halfway point. Just as I thought, she scolded, and warned him that his mind was an open book, one he might not want his grandchildren reading.

"Are you okay, Gram?" Joey asked.

"Yes, Joey. And so is Grandpa. Let's go see if we can find some wildflowers for your mom and Aunt Jeannie. You with me on this?"

"I know right where to go, Gram," and he was off like a shot.

"Wait up, Joey! I'm coming!" she shouted and sprinted across the meadow.

Chapter Twenty-five

"Steve! Steve! Wake up!" Megan whispered, shaking his arm.

"What? What's the matter?" Steve bolted upright, his heart thudding. "What is it? Are the kids all right?"

"Yes. They're asleep. I hear something. I'm scared!" Megan, usually a sound sleeper, was trembling.

He broke out into a cold sweat when he heard rustling bushes and the crunch of breaking branches. Jumping up, he quickly threw another log on the fire. It was almost daylight but fire might keep wild animals at bay. He could try to get the kids and Megan into a tree but the nearest limb was 20 feet from the ground.

"Megan," he whispered, "get in your sleeping bag and stay absolutely still."

"Oh God, Steve, I don't think I can do that."

"You can and you will," he ordered. "Get in your bag, now!"

Megan curled up in her bag, eyes wide and frightened. Steve found a sturdy branch, something he could use as a weapon, and stationed himself between his family and whatever was approaching. His heart pounded and his mouth was dry.

Whatever it was moved closer and stopped. There was total silence. Megan moved her head and Steve shot her a warning look. A final crunch sent his adrenaline pumping at top speed. A shadowy form began to take shape in the groove of young aspens. It was sleek and golden. It was a huge mountain lion.

Every muscle in Steve's body was coiled, ready to defend. He watched and waited, holding his breath until he nearly passed out.

He was sure no one would ever believe what happened next. Or why. The sleek cat, at least eight feet long, stepped into the clearing, its eyes never leaving Steve's face. It dropped a limp bundle of fur, what appeared to be a rabbit, on the ground, lowered its head, turned and walked away. Steve was stunned. It was an offering, a gift. Was it intentional or an accident? Had the animal given up its life because they were so hungry?

He pulled Megan out of her bag and held her close, telling her what he had witnessed. He showed her the rabbit carcass.

Megan's knees were shaking. "There's something very strange going on, Steve. I *know* my hands were bloody from climbing down the cliff but when I looked at them, they weren't bloody anymore. I thought I imagined it, but now this. There's a lesson in what just happened and we need to be aware of it."

"I'm not sure what's going on, either, honey, but nothing is the same anymore. I feel like layers of something around me are being unzipped, exposing feelings I never knew I had. Sort of what you're saying, Megan. Whatever it is, I like it."

"Me, too." She squeezed his hand, then reached up and gently touched his cheek. "I love you so much, Steve."

Warmth spread through him as he looked at his wife. She was surrounded with a soft pink light. He put his arms around her and kissed her tenderly. Another layer unzipped in his soul.

They thanked the mountain lion, the rabbit and their angels for their gift. Megan gathered sticks for skewers while Steve prepared the rabbit and woke up the boys. The appreciated meat sizzled in the hot fire and made their stomachs growl. They hadn't eaten food, let alone meat, in a long time, but this was obviously meant to be, to keep them alive. It felt right.

After their meal, they packed up, filled their canteens from the stream, and headed down the long dusty road.

Chris rolled over and slipped his arm around Ellen, pulling her close. Without Mary and Emma, he wasn't sure what to expect next. He wondered what was happening in the city. He hadn't heard any sirens or guns. His flesh and blood father had appeared out of thin air, so something was certainly different.

His sense of duty nagged at him. He really ought to drive into Raleigh and see if he was needed. He'd do it right now while the world was staying still and Ellen was sleeping. He wouldn't be gone long.

Disentangling himself, he quickly dressed, woke Ellen enough to tell her he'd be right back, grabbed his keys, and locked the door behind him.

He didn't get far. The car wouldn't start. It wouldn't even turn over. The office was a long walk away. The absolute quiet was eerie. There was no activity, no people.

He walked to the corner of his block, nearly bumping into an attractive woman hurrying by. She smiled, held out both hands, and said, "We made it, didn't we? Isn't this glorious? God was with us all the way. Now we'll have peace. Bless you, my friend." She crossed the street and Chris stared after her. He was dumbfounded. Normally people didn't to speak to strangers, at least not in this city.

Would there be peace or were they treading in two different dimensions for a while as Mary had suggested. Being in the Fifth, there was a choice. The Third still existed with its fear and violence, but where was it? If you made the cut, so to speak, were you part of both? It was crazy-making to think of it. He hoped Mary and Emma were okay, wherever they went, and that they'd keep in touch. There was much he needed to know.

Right now, given that he couldn't get to work, he thought of Ellen curled up in bed, cuddly as hell, waiting for him. That was the best place to be. They'd face the day together … later.

Julie watched from the deck as the high-spirited horses galloped across the meadow. Erica was snuggled in her lap and Joey was busy helping Grandpa mend fences. At her suggestion, Bill and Kathy agreed to exercise the animals. It wasn't much of a shove. They, as well as the horses, needed to release the pent-up emotions and energies of the last week.

It was a beautiful sight. Kathy's golden hair streamed out behind her, her laughter rippling through the air as Bill tried to overtake her. He had always loved speed but he had never ridden with such abandon.

The Shift had awakened the love he and Kathy had once shared. They now realized how much they really cared for each other and always had. The emotional gap had closed. The hidden barriers had melted along with the plastic goods. They were soul mates. Julie could see it in their eyes, in their auras. A healing had occurred, a new beginning.

Julie smiled as Bill and Kathy headed into the woods, holding hands.

~ ~ ~

Jean had recovered from childbirth unusually fast. She joined Julie on the deck and put an arm around her, resting her head on Julie's shoulder.

"How're you doing?" Julie asked.

"When I look at the baby, I'm so happy it scares me. Then I think about Jerry and my heart breaks."

"Do you have any gut feelings about what happened with Jerry?"

"He didn't make it, did he?"

"No, he didn't."

"What does that mean? Will I see him again? Why didn't he want to be with us?"

"It wasn't that he didn't want to be with you, Jeannie. He went into shock over Angela. He was overwhelmed with unnecessary guilt and feelings of inadequacy. He didn't have a trust and belief system in place. Jerry was filled with fear and simply unable to ascend into the Fifth. Spiritually, he wasn't ready. Will you see him again? I'm not sure. I've been told we can lower our vibrations down to the Third but those in that dimension can't raise theirs until they grow enough spiritually. My guess is that right now we're as invisible to him as he is to us."

"If I wanted to go back as you say, could I do it?" Jean asked.

"Eventually you might. But you must be very careful; you have a little baby to care for. At some point in the future, one of us will begin the search. I honestly don't know what we'll find. It's okay to mourn, Jeannie."

"I know," Jeannie sighed. "Everything you've said rings true in my heart. Jerry couldn't accept anything I'd learned spiritually.

It made me feel so alone, and now I am." Her eyes filled with tears.

"We'll all be there for you."

"I know."

"I thank God often that you're in my life this time around. I'll always think of you as my little girl."

"I like being 'your little girl.' Everyone needs a mother at times and I miss mine a lot. I love you, Julie," she said, squeezing her hand.

"I love you, too. Very much."

"Julie, do you remember when we thought we had tapped into some past lives together when we were tipping the table? I was real skeptical but it was fun."

"I remember. How does it feel to know that what we felt then was the truth? Can you sense the times we were together and what we learned from it? We've been friends many, many times before. That must be why we connected so easily this time. It's not a mother-daughter relationship as much as deep friendship. I like that. Maybe we're using that other ninety percent of the brain that science has wondered about."

"That would make sense, wouldn't it?" Jean pondered the possibility. "I have complete understanding of the meaning of all my relationships, why we came together, why we struggled. It's not painful; it feels good. I even feel—know—who Angela is—was—is. I think you're aware of it, too, Julie. I don't know how to say this, but I even know why she came to us the way she did."

"I couldn't tell you this at the time but when I first held your daughter and looked into her eyes, I connected with my Danny. I thought I might be projecting it because of the birth defect. But some part of his soul has returned. She's not Danny; she's Angela. Reincarnation is fascinating. Without a doubt, she is a very special young lady. With a very special mother, I might add."

Chapter Twenty-six

The winding trail through the woods appeared to be endless to Jesse as they walked along single file. He was preoccupied, unaware of the majestic mountain view, the cool, damp early morning, or the lizards scurrying across the path. Jesse was uncomfortable, not just from hunger and thirst, but from the bizarre dreams he'd been having for some time. Last night had been the strangest of all. He hadn't told anyone about it. His parents would tell him he had an over-active imagination. One time he'd tried to tell them about being able to fly at night, that he could go wherever he wanted; even visit Gram and Grandpa in Takoma Springs. They'd looked at each other, and then suggested he not eat just before bed, as though that had something to do with it. He didn't mention the dreams again.

Last night had felt real, too real. He'd gone for a ride on a space machine, some kind of flying saucer or ship. The people looked weird but were nice. They didn't speak out loud; he simply knew what they were saying and he talked to them the same way.

The first time he'd met them in his dreams, he'd been scared to death but, when he woke up, he was in his bed, in his own home. Last night, though, was different.

He remembered what they'd told him, like a lesson at school. The tall one, a male he thought, told him about the earth changes, things that Jesse had experienced in the cave. He explained why it had happened and that living in the new dimension would be exciting and sometimes confusing. So far, the dream teacher was right.

Jesse glanced at his parents. They were talking to each other, oblivious of the rest of the world.

"I don't want them to hear my thoughts," he muttered to himself, kicking a stone off the path.

Mike turned to him. "What'd you say?"

"Nothing. Just talking to Rusty."

"Oh." Mike wasn't up for arguing. He was thinking about a Big Mac and a soda.

We will put a veil of protection over your thoughts, Jesse. You are safe.

"What?"

"Oh. I just said oh," Mike answered.

"I thought I heard you say something."

"Well, I didn't."

That was strange. Jesse could have sworn he heard something.

You did, Jesse. You heard us. We're here with you now.

He stopped dead in his tracks. Rusty bumped into his legs and wagged his tail.

"Who's here?" Jesse asked, whispering so Mike wouldn't hear him. "Where are you?"

It's okay, Jesse. We spoke with you last night on the spaceship. We are here now to remind you of what we taught you. We will be your teachers, bring the memories back to you. If you look closely, you can see us now but we don't want to manifest and frighten the rest of your family. Here, beside you.

The voice echoed in his head, and he glanced around. He saw a hazy cloud on the left.

Yes, that's us. You'd better keep walking, by the way.

He'd fallen behind but no one seemed to notice.

Don't worry, Jess. They're focused on survival at the moment. They're thinking Third and Fourth Dimensionally and haven't opened up to all the ramifications of being in the Fifth. They will. Let's take it in stages since at some point, no doubt, you all want to be in your home. Your earth home. Sometime soon you can visit your past homes, too.

"What homes? I've always lived right here in Boulder."

In your past lives you've lived on other planets.

"Hey, whoever you are, this is getting too weird!"

Sorry, Jesse. We just want to help. Think about this: Can you get your family to manifest something easy, like food and water? When you take your next break, see what you can do. Use the word 'pray.' They're familiar with that. After that's been created, we'll help you manifest something spectacular. You can do it. You must do it if you want your family to remain in the new dimension. Fear is a big emotion and must be put to rest, once and for all.

Jesse knew what he heard was true. It was hard being a young boy and an old soul at the same time. It felt good having a Guardian Angel at his shoulder, no matter how out-of-this-world it might be.

The hours sped by. Soon the little mountain caravan pulled up for a pit stop. The hunger pangs were getting worse.

"We've got to find some food and water pretty soon," Steve said. "We've got to ration our supplies to make them last as long as we can. Drink some water but save some for later, okay?"

Jesse tried his two bites of rabbit meat. "Ugh! Boy, this is tough."

"I'll eat it if you don't want it," Mike offered.

"No thanks. I'll get it down," Jesse said, chewing hard. "Dad, Mom, can we try something?"

"What?" Megan asked.

"I think that if we picture what we want hard enough, we'll get it. It's called manifesting, that's it. If you picture something and pray and see yourself enjoying it, it will manifest. We should all do it together. It's more powerful if we all try it."

"It certainly can't do any harm, Jess," Steve said. "Let's form a circle and hold hands. We prayed in the cave. We can pray here, too."

They sat in a circle on a bed of pine needles and held hands.

"Okay, Jesse, what do you want to visualize?" Megan asked.

He closed his eyes. "Let's all think about having a big glass of water. It's cold and wet in our hands. Let's drink it up."

"It makes me too thirsty," Mike objected.

"Just be quiet and do it, Mikey," Jesse said. His authority surprised them. They became very quiet and did as they were told.

They visualized glasses of water. They lifted the glasses to their lips and drank deeply. It ran down their throats, filled their bellies, and quenched their thirst.

"When you're done drinking, say, 'Thank you, God'," Jesse directed. "Now picture some food. Let's see. Let's visualize eating something, really tasting it, and saying, 'Oh boy, this is good!' That way we don't limit how it will happen—ah—manifest."

They thanked God for the blessings, shook off the pine needles and stretched their legs. They waited a few moments, but nothing materialized. “Okay, guys,” said Steve, patting Jesse on the back. “Let’s hit the trail again. Sorry it didn’t work, Jess.”

“Yeah,” said Jesse. He wasn’t sure what he expected but he’d at least followed directions.

Half an hour later, they broke through the dense forest into a meadow.

Megan saw it first. “Hey, look! There’s a cabin!” In a burst of energy, they ran up to the door.

“Hello! Anybody home?” Steve asked, knocking. “Hello! Please, if you’re home, we need some help.”

When they received no answer, they walked around to the back. Megan saw it first.

“Look, Steve! There’s a well. Jesse! Michael! Maybe we can get some water.”

“It’s probably deep and we won’t be able to reach it,” Steve said.

“Oh, don’t be so negative, Steve. Let’s look,” Megan said, heading for the well. She lifted the worn wooden top. “There’s a rope and a bucket here. Come on, let’s try it.”

Steve tossed the wooden bucket down and pulled up some of the clearest, most sparkling water they’d ever seen. They dug out their metal cups and drank until they could hold no more. Refreshed, they filled their canteens. The day was beautiful once again.

“There’s food inside,” Jesse announced.

“There isn’t anyone at home,” Megan said. “We can’t just break in.”

“We’re supposed to go inside,” Jesse insisted. “Maybe the door is open. Let’s try.”

"It's probably been abandoned for a long time so don't get your hopes up," Steve warned.

Boy, Jesse thought, it's gonna be hard to change *his* way of thinking.

They went to the back door and turned the handle. It was old and squeaky but it moved. They pushed the door open and Steve stepped inside, followed by his family. The cabin was empty except for a well-used antique rocker and a small stained wooden table. Wide board pine floors creaked as Steve investigated. It hadn't been occupied for a long time and dust and cobwebs were everywhere. Much to their surprise, they discovered several cans of food covered with a layer of dust on the kitchen counter. Next to them lay a can opener.

"Wow!" Mike said, grabbing a can of green beans. "Food! Real food! I could eat a horse!"

"No, you couldn't," Jesse scolded, "so don't even say that."

"Jeez! Don't get all ticked, Jesse. I was just kidding."

"Well, don't kid like that. You'd better take this manifesting seriously. Look what we did already."

"Oh, my goodness, you're right!" Megan exclaimed. "Do you suppose … ?" She looked closely at her son.

"We'd better not look a gift horse in the mouth, guys," Steve said. "However this got here, coincidence or not, it will save our lives."

He looked around the kitchen and slowly walked to the corner cabinet and opened it. On the first shelf was a jar of peanut butter. He picked it up, unscrewed the top and smelled it. "It's fresh. This is fresh peanut butter! You're not going to believe this, but when we were visualizing eating and drinking, a jar of peanut butter came to my mind and I put it in a cupboard just like … Oh my God! Did I put it here?"

"I think so, Dad," Jesse said. "That's what manifesting is all about."

The food would be enough for a few days. They left a note with their phone number, and thanked their benefactors for their generosity.

Closing up the cabin, they continued down the trail. Jesse didn't know what the next adventure would be, but it would be hard to top this one. It didn't matter. His hunger and thirst were gone and his dad was whistling. Smiling, he looked at the sky and winked.

Chapter Twenty-seven

This is really bizarre, Jon thought, walking through the streets of San Francisco. The sky was brilliant and buildings were more whitewashed than ever. Storefronts and signs appeared to have been given a fresh coat of paint. It was quiet, incredibly silent. He wasn't complaining, but there was something missing. He just hadn't keyed into it yet.

Occasionally he passed someone and they exchanged friendly greetings. That was unbelievable. It just didn't happen in the City. There used to be thousands of people who lived a much different life than what Jon was seeing now. Peace and love and beauty surrounded him. He wondered what happened to the rest of the world.

Jon walked to the Marina. It was uncluttered and quiet. He climbed over the breakwater and sat on a flat rock above the spray. Being near the ocean had always been important to him and, although he'd been warned of the dangers from earth changes to the waterfront, he always seemed to be in a safe place at the right time. Now the ocean was at peace, too. Clear and clean and cold. He stared across the gently rolling swells to where the Golden Gate Bridge had been. It gave him a chill to see the bent and twisted orange towers that had once soared into the heavens. The cables and the road span angled down into the hungry waters of San Francisco Bay, a grotesque reminder of the Big Quake.

"You're in your light-body now, Jon," a voice said.

He looked around, startled. He saw nothing.

"I'm out here, Jon."

"Where? Who? I can hear you but I can't see you."

"I'm in the sea. One of the Mer People. You can hear and understand my language now, Jon. Everything has changed."

Mer People. The sea. He scanned the water before him. A most magnificent creature, the most beautiful dolphin he'd ever seen, looked up at him, a smile on his face.

"Welcome to the Fifth Dimension, Jon."

"I'll be damned."

"I wouldn't say that if I were you," the dolphin smiled.

"Ah, yeah. This is amazing. I'm talking with you. I hear dolphin chatter but I understand what you're saying. This is incredible. Do you know my thoughts or do I need to speak out loud?"

"What do you think, Jon? You're a light-being now and so are we. Nothing will ever be the same for you. Congratulations."

"Well, thank you. Same to you." He paused for a moment. "Do you know what the devil's going on here in the city?"

"You know all about this sort of thing, Jon, on a level you haven't fully opened to yet. In a nutshell, to use one of your quaint phrases, what has occurred is that you have simply left the Third Dimension behind. It's still there but you're not part of it—unless you choose to be."

"Okay, Mister Dolphin. I understand that part."

"Please call me Ekor. We might as well be on a first name basis."

"Agreed, Ekor. Please continue."

"There are many beings in the human form that did not, could not, ascend. They were not spiritually ready; they refused to see the light. These people are all around you now, extremely frantic, frightened of what's happening, not understanding. The rape and pillage continues, the gang wars, the killings. The economy has collapsed. Government and the media are predicting doom and gloom for the world. That doesn't even touch on the spiritual emptiness pervading their very being."

"But I don't see that here. What city is it in? What country?"

"It's right here, all around you, but at a lower frequency," Ekor explained. "You can't see it because at the moment you don't accept that you *can*. If it is your desire, you can lower your vibrations to that level and witness the violence and carnage taking place. You've been told this but it's a difficult concept to accept. That's why I'm here, to remind you. Knowing you, you'll want to jump back to the Third to help those beings, especially the children, who would be open to the words that will help shift them into the Fifth. Many will hear the message from light beings like you and make the Shift before it's too late. It will, no doubt, be both frustrating and rewarding. But you must remember one thing: They won't be able to see you unless you lower your vibrations to match theirs. You are invisible to them now, just as the Masters have been invisible to you. You've communicated with Higher Beings in your thoughts, through table-tipping, and legitimate channelers. Now you will actually see them in person. Third-Dimensional beings will not be able to see you or them. Sad but true." Ekor tossed his head. "Do you understand?"

"I think I do. You're saying that this city looks worse to hundreds, maybe thousands, of people who are still here right now. They're hearing sirens, seeing fires, blood and guts even as we speak?"

"You are correct."

"But those beings who have opened up spiritually, who were able to ascend, are seeing a whole different world—the one I'm seeing around me now? And the two worlds co-exist in the same space?"

"Right again. That's the way it is, Jon."

"Okay," Jon said. "Now. I can go back to the Third by willing myself there. Using my mind, the way I went to Takoma Springs?"

"Yes."

"I can't think of why I'd want to go there, Ekor."

"You will, Jon. You're a teacher. You've written books to help people grow, to motivate them to a better life. Your soul won't want to stop now. There are children caught in the in-between who need guidance to cross over. You can help them and you will. You can work through your dreams the way you've done before, if you wish. In many ways your work has just begun.

"That about covers today's lessons, Jon. Go forth with your heart. If you want to talk again, come back to the rock. I'll know. I'm off now. It's a wonderful day for a swim."

With a flip of his tail, Ekor dove into the deep blue water, and then surfaced, expressing his joy with a perfect somersault, creating a splash that sparkled with rainbows before disappearing into the San Francisco Bay.

Jon stared after his new friend. Breakers crashed on the shore and seagulls swooped and soared overhead, cawing to one another. Everything *looked* normal.

Jon stood and stretched, then made his way over the rocks back to his apartment. What he really needed, he decided, was to find others to talk with who were in a similar place of understanding—a group, a family with whom to share the extraordinary Photon experience.

He considered a quick trip to Wind Dancer Ranch but rejected the idea. He'd chosen to make his home by the ocean, knowing he'd be where he needed to be when it was appropriate. When Spirit said to kick butt, he'd do it.

"Yes, sir, Spirit, if you've got something to say, say it. Guide me. I could use a little direction right now."

No sooner had he uttered his request than he felt a presence nearby. He saw a handsome young man with long hair and a beard wearing a T-shirt and a baseball cap walking towards him.

"Morning," Jon said.

"Morning, Jon. Incredible day, isn't it?" The stranger smiled warmly.

"How did you know my name?" Jon looked into the stranger's eyes and knew in his heart he was no stranger. "I … you're … I know who you are," Jon said, stumbling for words. "I'm sorry. I just don't know what to say. I would have expected you to be dressed … differently. You look like, you know, a regular guy. I guess you're here because I asked for help, right?"

"Yes, Jon. I can be anywhere I'm needed. Robes aren't in style anymore, you know? I heard your plea for help. Trust yourself, Jon. You already know what to do, and where. Just be open to it and the information will flow. Pay attention to your dreams. They're powerful. Your work is important during the night, so that's a wonderful place to start. Focus on the children. You treat them with respect and as small adults. So many will need that now. Remember that there are many of us here to help for the asking. You and I have worked together before and we will once again. God bless you, Jon. Go in God's light." The man disappeared into thin air.

In a daze, Jon headed for home. He had much to contemplate, much to understand and accept. It wasn't every day that one got to talk with Jesus of Nazareth.

Jon sat on the edge of his bed. He had always been in touch with the world and his place in it, but now his ego had been stripped away. He didn't possess the words to explain it, but there was a purity of thought, an understanding of enormous concepts he hadn't known were there. He wavered between tears and laughter, wanting to share it with someone yet needing to be alone to savor the flow of awareness and love that filled him. He rolled around once or twice, appreciating the feel of bedclothes, his own body, the sense of peace within and without. Within minutes he was asleep.

Jon became aware that he was lucid dreaming. Children's Hospital, his first stop, glowed in the distance. Joy rippled through the walls and rooftop and the sound of laughter was better than any music he'd ever heard. Roger, who had been bald and within two weeks of dying, was laughing at the antics of Phillip, who was using his crutches as toys. Roger kept running his fingers through the thatch of golden curls on his head. When he saw Jon, he leaped out of bed and threw his arms around his tall friend who told funny stories.

"Jon! Jon! Look! Look at me! I'm walking—and I've got hair! I'm not sick any more!"

"Hey, dude, that's super! Looks like you're not alone, either. Tell me what happened."

"It was scary. I thought we were dying. It got so dark and cold and we couldn't see and we were alone. I mean, a couple of nurses were here but they couldn't see, either, and they were really scared. But I remembered how you used to tell me to never be afraid, and about God and angels and everything. So I just started talking to Him and asked Him to help us, me and my friends. Then this light started to fill the room. I couldn't tell where it was coming from but it felt so good. Someone started talking to me in my head, saying the things you used to say, and this nurse that I'd never seen before walked in. She gave us hugs and everything. She said things like, 'you are healing. You'll run and play soon.' Stuff like that. The next thing I knew, it was morning and the sun was coming out again. And I had hair!"

"Hey, that's great," Jon said, enjoying the happy exuberance of his buddies.

"And I looked at the other kids and everyone looked different. We started getting out of bed and we *could!* My head feels like it's swimming. I can even tell what some of the others are thinking sometimes. It's weird! Do you think my Mom and Dad will come soon? I can't wait to go home and see Missy, my cat, and ride my bike and everything. It's a miracle, isn't it, Jon!" he said, his eyes shining in joy and wonderment.

"Yes, Roger, it is. A really big one and what's happened to you is one of the best parts. You and your friends have made a major transition. You've ascended into a higher dimension, a beautiful level of vibrations where there is no sickness, only love. There are many things to learn."

Jon smiled and ruffled Roger's hair. "I bet your parents will get here as soon as they can. They went through the same kind of experience you did, but the world is different out there now. I think they were ready to make the leap into the Fifth, too, but they might not realize they can travel in different ways now. It might take a little time. It's probably good for you to know that some folks just weren't able to open their minds to what could manifest for them so they have chosen to remain in the Third Dimension. That's where we were before. A lot of them will learn to trust in God and that's where you kids come in. You're going to be teachers for a lot of adults when you get home, Roger. Do you understand what I'm saying?"

"I guess so, yeah. It's gonna be pretty confusing."

"You've got that right, Roger. Just keep your mind open to all possibilities. I'm still learning myself, but I'll be back again to see how you're doing, okay?"

"But I won't be here! How are you going to find me?"

"That's one of the special changes, Roger. I'll find you no matter where you are. And you'll be able to visit me the same way. Just *poof!* and we can be together for a while. How's that sound?"

"That sounds cool, Jon! I can't wait!"

"In the meantime, remember that special nurse who came when it was dark?"

"Yeah. Where is she?"

"She's here for you any time you need her. Just ask God for help. Let Him know it's important and she or another angel will take care of you."

Roger got real quiet. "Was she an angel?"

"Yup. You'll begin to see them all around you soon. You'll see relatives and friends who have passed over. They can now reappear with the new energies. It may be startling, but know that it's okay. That's the way it's supposed to be."

"Am I dead, Jon? Am I in heaven now?" he asked with a very concerned look on his face.

"Oh no! You're very much alive, more than you've ever been before. You'll get to enjoy a lot of very special new things, Roger."

"Okay. My dead grandma might come back?" His forehead wrinkled in thought. "She's not dead and I might see her again?"

"Yup. She was never dead, just in a different form. She'll reappear when the time is right. Just keep her in your thoughts and talk to her. Okay, buddy?"

"Okay."

"So, my friend, I hate to leave but I've got a lot of work to do tonight. How about if I look for you in a few days? I'll stop in to say hi to you and Missy."

"Hey, that would be great! I love you, Jon. Thanks for coming."

"Bye, Roger. I love you, too."

Roger sat on the bed after Jon left, his head tipped to one side, deep in thought.

Chapter Twenty-eight

Sparks exploded high above the bonfire at Wind Dancer Ranch as the wood crackled and spat. The fragrant meadow glowed and stars twinkled overhead. Flames lit up their faces as Dave and Julie began harmonizing the hymn, *Let There Be Peace On Earth.* By the time they started the second verse, friends began joining in, some walking across the field, some simply appearing by the fire, holding hands or with arms around each other. It was a joyful reunion of souls coming together once again, souls who now were aware of their many lifetimes together. Dave and Julie had been successful in sending their mental invitations.

After the song, someone put a hand on Julie's arm. "Anna! Doug! You got the message!"

"We felt you'd made it home, Dave," Doug said. "Was it rough getting here?"

"It sure felt that way. I'll fill you in later. Come meet our newest granddaughter who arrived along with the Shift. Now *that* was a night!"

More and more people gathered around the fire. Julie suggested they hold hands to connect their energies and increase the power of their prayers. She led them through a relaxing meditation, and then addressed the Prime Source, the Mother-Father-God within and without, asking to be heard. "Please hear our prayers of thanks for your guidance and your love and protection. We know you are with us, always around us, in us, in everything, but we want to express our gratitude and our love, too. The Fifth Dimension is …"

As she spoke, a rich and powerful voice joined in, speaking her thoughts. It was deep and she could feel the vibration of it. Julie lowered her voice to a whisper, and then stopped talking altogether as the resonant tones took over.

"… is a most beautiful loving place to be, dear ones. Because of your unconditional trust in a Higher Power, you have begun the Ascension process. I will always be with you and all living things. Continue on your paths; accept with wonder the extraordinary experiences of your new world, new friends and old friends. What you believe will be granted to you, but do not forget to help those less fortunate and continue to better the world in which you live."

Everyone, including the children, was mesmerized by this being whose aura illuminated them all, this unknown energy that touched their souls.

"I must leave you now. I give you my blessings and my love. Peace. Be Still."

The energy slowly withdrew, leaving an afterglow of white light behind. No one moved or spoke for a long time.

"It was a manifestation of the Holy Spirit," Joey said quietly.

As soon as Julie found her voice again, she suggested they perform a group healing for the world and all beings in and upon it. Standing in a circle around the fire, they joined hands once again and bowed their heads.

"Mother, Father, God," Julie began, "we wish to send a healing to all living things on our beautiful planet Earth and beyond. We also send special healing and love to those beings who remain in the Third and Fourth Dimensions, knowing it is their choice to receive or reject this healing. Thank you again for your protection, your guidance, your ever-loving presence and everlasting light. So be it."

As the fire died away, the assemblage exchanged warm embraces and bid their farewells. Some chose to walk under the stars while others beamed themselves home.

Dave put his arm around Julie as they headed up the path, lost in their own thoughts and in each other's.

The campfire deep in the mountains of Colorado cast lingering shadows across the tent walls. Crickets and frogs serenaded Steve and Megan as they snuggled in the afterglow of their own passionate fire. Barriers had been shattered and they knew each other as never before.

Jesse and Mike slept soundly in their pup tent, enjoying a sense of safety and protection. It had been a long but satisfying day. Their newfound ability to manifest what they needed to survive was empowering.

Steve thought it was strange how they could read each other's thoughts. It was almost like a game, although it was hard to know whose thoughts they were tapping into. All except for Jesse. When Steve tried to tune into his thoughts, it was like hitting a one-way phone line. Jesse could dial out but he didn't accept incoming calls.

Mike dreamed of his bicycle at home and the playground at school. Jesse, on the other hand, was aware of being on another out-of-body adventure. The really fun dreams were when he soared among the stars. He could do anything an acrobat at the circus did but he never fell down. He somersaulted, twisted and turned, defied gravity by floating on his back, or zipped around like Superman. Sometimes he was alone; other times he had company but was never sure who or what.

Jesse remembered one trip where he landed on a different planet and was greeted by beings who welcomed him with open arms. Everything was covered in a blue haze, even the inhabitants, but it felt right and he was comfortable. He felt more at home there than in his own house. He'd been sorry to wake up from that dream.

Tonight he was lifting off again, soaring swiftly upward with a purpose. He felt he was dreaming, yet experiencing and observing at the same time. It pleased him to see that his companion was the invisible teacher who had joined him on the trail.

"Hi!" Jesse said.

"Hi to you, too, Jess. Grand night for a flight, to soar out of sight with all of your might."

"Oh, brother," Jesse said with a touch of disgust.

"Sorry. Just trying to lighten you up a bit. Life's a bit tense on planet Earth right now."

"It's okay. Dad always says I need to laugh more. He's probably right."

"You're entitled. Who you are and what you're experiencing would be incomprehensible to him at the moment. Your brother is growing up, too."

"Not fast enough for me," Jesse laughed. "Do you have a name?"

"Of course. Several, as a matter of fact. So let's see. What would be appropriate for you to call me?" He thought for a moment. "Okay, how about Dorado? Does that resonate with you?"

"Dorado. Dorado. It's different but I think I can get used to it. So, Dorado, where are we going?"

"A ship. A very large space ship. You'll like it. I can't wait to show it to you."

"How big?" Jesse asked.

"You'll see. Won't be long now."

Jesse observed the stars flying by, felt the air whoosh around him as they sped ahead. He stopped in mid-flight.

"Holy shit!" he exclaimed as an enormous object materialized in front of him.

"I beg your pardon?" Dorado said.

"Sorry. What is it? It's huge!"

"This is one of many ships in your universe. This is a teaching ship. People like you, and some who aren't like you, come here during dreamtime to learn and practice the things they need to help guide others in their growth. You're not just your body. Your soul encompasses much more. Your soul can be inside your body on earth but it can be elsewhere, too, communicating with others on the earth plane or in a higher dimension. Am I making sense to you, Jesse?"

"I think so. How long will we be here and what's it like inside?"

"That's your earthly left brain kicking in," Dorado laughed. "Just relax and enjoy the experience. Believe me, you won't be missed in your tent and you'll be back in time for breakfast."

The gleaming white ship was several miles long. On board, all communication was telepathic, something Jesse was getting used to. He found himself in a very strange classroom. Some of his classmates had colored skin; some were bald. Others had scaly skin like lizards. He saw beings that reminded him of the pictures he'd seen of the Roswell incident. Many of the students' energies were familiar but there wasn't time to renew old friendships. One of the teachers said the Photon energy had stirred up a lot of activity and this was a crash training course.

A beautiful glowing being, a "Lady Angel" as Jesse would later describe in his notebook, guided them into a trance state. She explained that they would be given a transference of energy and information they would retain and share with others when needed.

Jesse noticed the beings around him had each become a glow of light, and he felt as though he had no body. Then his thoughts disappeared.

When he became aware of his body again, it was solidifying and Dorado was sitting next to him. He tentatively shook his arms and legs.

"As soon as you gather your energies together, Jesse, we'll head back to your world."

Jesse looked at Dorado as though seeing his friend for the first time. A new level of understanding had evolved between them. Jesse now possessed an awareness of the past, the present, and the future. It was neither the first nor the last time that they would work together.

The return flight was uneventful and quick. Jesse simply followed the silver cord, the ethereal umbilical cord that kept him connected to his body.

His cosmic friend sent a final message. *Jesse, use the knowledge you've been given tonight with love, compassion, and joy. Sleep in peace, my dear friend. I'll always be near you. I love you.*

Jesse smiled as he rolled over in his sleeping bag. He spent the rest of the night in a dreamless sleep.

"Rise and shine, boys! The dawn is breaking and it's time to face the world once again," Steve said.

Both boys groaned and burrowed deeper into their warm nests.

"Come on, guys. I've got some hot tea ready to warm your bones and Mom has made breakfast from the food we have left. Smells a bit like peanut butter," he added, hoping that would get their attention. It did. "So how did you sleep, boys? There weren't any mountain lions or other critters around that we were aware of."

"It was okay," Mike said, yawning, "but I want to go home. I dreamed about school and my friends and I miss them. Will we get home soon, Dad?"

"I don't know, Mikey. We've got a long way to go before we reach the main road and who knows what we'll find there. But we'll get there sooner or later. Chin up, tiger. How was your night, Jess?"

Jesse hung his head. "Fine." He wasn't ready to share his strange experience yet.

"How about your dreams? Did you dream of school and your friends?"

"Sort of. I guess you could say that."

Breakfast over, they loaded up their packs and headed down the trail with Rusty in the lead. They followed a brook, a delightfully refreshing sound.

Jesse brought up the rear, lost in thought. He kept hearing the words, *Soon, Jesse. Do it soon*, but he wasn't sure what he was supposed to do.

Thoughts of his grandmother flooded his mind. He could see her in his third eye, smell her perfume, hear her laugh. He could almost feel her presence and longed to be with her. She would understand.

Chapter Twenty-nine

Julie, a steaming cup of tea in hand, escaped the after-breakfast activity in the kitchen and nestled in her favorite spot on the deck. She had been uneasy for the last half hour. Her thoughts kept drifting to Steve and his family. She wondered where they were and if they were all right.

Leaning her head against the side of the house, she closed her eyes, allowing the warmth of the sun to seep through her body. Uninvited, a form began to take shape in her third eye. Someone was calling in, nudging her.

"Jesse!" she whispered, recognizing her grandson. A strong vibrational connection raced through the ethers, one she wouldn't have expected. So he's the one. He's the teacher, the little Master up north.

She tuned into his thoughts and experienced complete knowing instantly. Now that the connection was made, she could easily find them in the Rockies. Without a second thought, she focused on her grandson sitting on a log by the river, and much to her surprise and delight, she materialized beside him.

"Gramma!" Jesse's eyes filled with love and he threw his arms around her neck. Steve turned at the sound and saw Julie. At least he thought he did. He simply sat there, mouth open, wondering if he was hallucinating.

"Megan," he whispered, "do you see what I see?"

Megan followed his gaze and let out a gasp. "I see your mother!" she cried in disbelief. In a daze they stared at the apparition as though it might disappear.

"It's okay, Mom and Dad. It's really Gramma. She's real." He glowed with a young boy's pride and delight.

Julie ran to her son and embraced him. He buried his face on her shoulder. She opened one arm to include Megan in the group hug and all three wept tears of joy.

Jesse ran to the edge of the creek bank. "Mikey, come quick! Gramma Julie's here!"

Mike looked up from his fishing, a frown of sheer disgust on his face. This was not the time for that kind of joke. It wasn't even funny.

"Honest, Mike! Come on. See for yourself."

Reluctantly, Mike climbed up the rocky hillside, curiosity getting the best of him. His eyes widened when he saw the threesome with their arms around each other.

"Gramma! Gramma!" he shouted, throwing himself against her legs. Julie disentangled herself from the group and picked Mike up for a hug.

They sat in a circle on a bed of pine needles by the creek and Julie brought them up to date on the Photon experience in Takoma Springs. She told the boys about their new cousin and the angel who helped deliver her. She told them about Joey and the goat and more. Then the campers shared their story of life in the cave and after, about the mountain lion and the cabin, and their concerns for survival.

"There's one thing I don't understand, Mom, and that's how the devil you got here," Steve said. "How did you know where to find us and how did you do it?"

"Jesse called me telepathically. I picked up on his energy and was able to connect."

A grandson nestled in each arm, everyone's thought forms bombarded her mind and she struggled to turn off the telepathic switch. But one stream of consciousness kept penetrating her awareness. It came from Jesse. Instructions of some sort but not the kind she would expect from a six-year-old child.

While Steve and Megan packed up supplies, Mike went to check his hastily made fishing pole he'd left by the creek to see if he'd caught anything. Julie claimed she needed to stretch her legs and invited Jesse to come along for company. Hand in hand, they walked up the dusty trail.

Jesse was finally able to share his strange dreams. He told her about Dorado and the huge space ship, about going to school at night, and flying in the heavens.

"I'm so proud of you, Jesse. You've been given so much information and you've handled it all in a very grown-up way," Julie reassured him. "But remember, you're still a young boy. You don't need to take on the responsibilities of the world just yet. Take things one step at a time as your awareness grows, and do what feels right to you."

"But, Gramma, there's some way I'm supposed to help Mom and Dad get out of here and I don't know what it is!" he cried. "I can't remember from the dream."

"I think I know what it is, Jesse. It's not about the trail or a car or anything like that. We need to help your parents and Mike understand how to trans-locate, how to do what I did to get here. Anyone can do it but they need to believe they can do it in order to achieve it. You're all capable of doing it now. The experience you all had in that cave helped push your family along into the Fifth Dimension faster than might otherwise have happened."

"That's for sure!" Jesse said emphatically. "But I don't know how to do that trans-locating thing."

"Remember when you were concentrating on me, the longing you felt to see me again? That's what's needed. Let's see if you and I can teach the others how to do that. I don't think it'll be a problem, do you?"

"No. We really want to go home. But what about Rusty?"

"I'm not sure but I bet if you talk to him and all form a tight circle around him, you'll all travel together. It might surprise Rusty but he'll go, too. Believe me, Rusty understands more than you think."

When they returned to his family, Jesse called for a family meeting. "I know how to get us home to Boulder, even Rusty. We can do what Gramma did and think ourselves there, right, Gramma?"

Julie nodded, smiling.

"That's stretching it a bit, Mom. What happens if we don't all make it?" asked Steve.

"Not to worry, guys. I'll wait until you're all gone. Then Jesse can connect with me to let me know you're safe and sound."

They formed a circle around Rusty and focused their thoughts on the lush grass by the newly planted apple tree in their back yard. They utilized all their senses to make it real. At Julie's suggestion, each said, "I am there."

Her family evaporated before her eyes, traveling through time and space to arrive next to the apple tree, Rusty included.

All were giddy with the joy of being home, all except Jesse who sat quietly and connected with his grandmother through his third eye. He saw her smile, felt the words, "Congratulations" and "I love you," and then his screen went blank.

With Angela snuggled in her arms, Jeannie sat on the edge of the swiftly-flowing creek behind the house, basking in the sunshine and marveling at the clear blue water sparkling and gurgling around the rocks. Thanks to the newly found brook, she was able to keep up with the laundry and diapers. She experienced a gratifying sense of accomplishment.

Jerry's absence left an aching hole in her heart, but the support of her family helped ease the pain. For the first time in her life, she knew what "living in the now" meant.

"Where on earth did this water come from?" Julie said, interrupting Jean's reverie.

"What do you mean, Julie? Is this something new?"

"Yes. This is was a dry creek. It flowed when the snow melted or there were heavy rains but even then it never looked like this. It's beautiful! It's fantastic!"

"All I know is that I was trying to figure out how to handle Angela's dirty diapers with very little water and no washing machine. Then I found this brook and hauled buckets of water to that big old tub by the barn. It worked well enough. I didn't even stop to ask how come it was here."

"Of course!" Julie exclaimed, "It's so simple. Faith and trust. Total belief that what we need will manifest. What an impressive example. You didn't question how, you just said thank you to the universe and hung the laundry on the clothesline. Perfect! I love it! Good work, Jeannie!" She unlaced her shoes and dangled her feet in the cold mountain water.

"Would you like to hold Angela for a while?" Jean asked.

Julie's smile answered the question and she gently placed the baby in Julie's arms. Angela opened her eyes and stared into her grandmother's eyes. They both knew it wasn't a gas bubble that lifted the corners of her rosebud mouth.

Joey ran across the field toward Julie and Jean, tears slicing through the mud on his cheeks. He thrust out a bloody knee and said, "The goat did it! I tried to ride her the way Daddy rides a horse but she ran and I fell and look what she did!"

"Let me see it, Joey," Julie said. "I bet that was frustrating for you but Daisy Mae's never had anyone sit on her back before. I expect you gave her a good scare. You know, getting hurt like that is pretty Third-Dimensional, but I bet you know how to fix this in a hurry. Can you tell me how?"

"What do you mean, Gramma? Can I make this go away all by myself? Right now?"

"Remember what you were doing for Aunt Jeannie the other night when she was giving birth?"

"You mean using my hands like you do?" His forehead wrinkled in puzzlement.

"Yes, Joey. You can run energy. You've done it before. It's even easier now. Let's give it a try. I'll help you."

Joey took a deep breath and let it out slowly. "Okay, Gram. I'm ready."

He sat cross-legged in front of Julie and closed his eyes.

"I want you to relax, Joey. This isn't hard work. God does the work. You're just a channel for the energy to come through and out your hands. Feel it come in through the top of your head. Let it go down your arms and out the palms of your hands right onto the bruise. Use your imagination. See your knee healing, the skin repairing itself, the blood drying up. Picture your knee healthy like the other one. Know that it doesn't hurt anymore and that you can run and play again."

With a child's natural ability to "make believe," Joey had no problem following directions. His hands felt hot, really hot, and so did the skin on his knee. When Julie said the knee was healed and that he could check it out for himself, he opened his eyes. Lifting his thumbs, he peeled back his hands as though releasing a great secret and stared at his healed knee. He brushed away the dried blood. The knee was healed.

"I did it, Gramma! Did you see that, Aunt Jeannie? It's all better! How did I do that?"

"There's so much you can do, Joey. You have no idea yet how many gifts you have. I know you're a big boy but I suggest you stay off Daisy Mae. Maybe you can take a ride with your dad on Orion. But first, let me clean up that face of yours."

She dipped a hanky in the water and cleaned his tear-streaked cheeks. He grimaced and, at the first opportunity, trotted off for the barn.

"Sure wish Nana Rose could be here to see the baby," Jean said. "It's too bad healing like that didn't work back then. I miss her so much, Julie."

"I do, too. I was very connected to your grandmother in past lives as well as this one. She has always been around you and your dad, especially since she died. As a matter of fact, I feel her presence very strongly right now. How about really concentrating on her? Bring her into your thoughts and make her as real as you can.

You need each other and I think you might be surprised by what could happen. Want to try it?"

Jean nodded. Julie kissed her on the cheek and left her to her privacy.

As Julie climbed the steps to the deck, Dave came out to meet her. Before he could say anything, she placed a finger on his lips, put her arm around him, and pointed to Jean sitting by the brook. They watched as a form slowly began to materialize beside her. They saw the incredulous look on Jean's face as she reached out her hand to her beloved Nana. Dave took a step forward when he recognized his mother but Julie held him back.

"Shhh. Let them have some time. Rose will be here for us, too, but this is a special moment, meeting her great-granddaughter. And Jeannie needs her so much."

"I can't believe what I'm seeing, Julie. It's my mother! I know we were told it could happen but I never thought I'd really see her again, or my dad. Do you realize my dad will be able to meet you in person for the first time?"

"I know and I can't wait. But let's take it one step at a time and savor the wonder of it all. Look," Julie said, nodding toward the threesome.

Jean was holding out her child, her eyes never leaving the face of the woman who had surrounded her with so much love.

Chapter Thirty

"Ellen, I can't find my gun," Chris said, coming into the bedroom. "I know I left it on the counter but it's not there. Did you put it away somewhere?"

"You know I wouldn't touch that thing!" Ellen climbed out of bed and shrugged on her robe. "Are you sure that's where you left it? You went out yesterday. Did you take it with you?"

"No. At least I don't think so. This is too weird. How can someone who enforces the law walk around unarmed, for Pete's sake!" Chris followed her into the kitchen.

"Calm down, Chris. Let's think this through. Mary and Emma could probably explain it. I really miss them."

"Seems like a lifetime ago, doesn't it? Amazing how we've changed, Ellen, how the world has changed. I feel like I'm living in two places at once. I wonder where Mary is. Maybe I can find her downtown, where I picked them up. Think I should go look?"

"No, don't even think about it," Ellen warned, searching the cupboards for something they could eat cold. Chris followed in her footsteps. "Anyway, I think it's much easier than that. Your dad just up and thought himself here, so what would happen if we concentrate on Mary?"

She settled on a can of corn and cranked it open. Chris wrinkled his nose. "I don't want us to go anywhere but maybe she can talk to us, you know, through our minds or something.

We've nothing to lose, Chris. Besides," she added scowling, "if you step out that door, I'll be glued to you like a shadow."

Chris grinned. "Yeah, I figured you'd feel that way. I won't go anywhere without you, not yet anyway."

He found a pile of potato chips lose on the shelf and frowned. "There's some missing link we haven't figured out yet. Things like guns and holsters don't just disappear. What the heck, let's give Mary a shot."

"Bad choice of words," Ellen laughed. "How about calling her on the ethereal communication line."

They sat yoga fashion on the living room floor, held hands, and concentrated on their new friend. They visualized her sitting on their couch, talking with them once again. Releasing the mind chatter, they focused on their intense desire to make the connection. Her energy and words came to them, telepathically. "Hello, dear ones. I've missed you."

"Mary!" Chris said. "How are you and Emma?"

"We couldn't be better, my friends."

"Mary, there are so many strange things happening … or not happening. Can you help us understand?"

"Of course. Give me a moment. Ah, yes, you're concerned that you can't find your firearm. Is that it?"

"Yes," Chris said, amazed she could read their minds. "It seems inconsequential in the whole scheme of things but, yes, it's disappeared."

"Your firearm has remained in the Third Dimension. As you're aware, guns only made things worse, not better. You have no need for it now. Should you choose to go back to help others grow and perhaps ascend as you have, you won't need a gun to do it. You both have much to learn yet; we all have, for that matter. Trust your instincts, your intuition. Are you going to Colorado soon?"

"Sometime, yes," said Ellen. "It was wonderful seeing Chris' dad but we're not ready to project ourselves to another state yet. I mean, it's scary, just disappearing. What if we get lost out there? What if only one of us goes and the other gets stuck here?"

"Ellen, dear Ellen," Mary sighed. "I hear such fear in your voice. I would ask you to begin meditating together and asking for spiritual guidance. Try tuning into your folks in Colorado. Reach out to loved ones who have passed on. You can connect, but only if you believe and trust."

"We trust you," Ellen said. "I don't know what we'd have done without you."

"Gather your energies and power back in again. Bring it into yourself; fill yourself. Don't give it away to me or anyone or anything else. Your family's waiting for you back there. Go when you're ready." She paused. "Chris? Do you have any other questions? I'm always here to help you, you know."

"Thanks so much, Mary. Julie used to say that the information would be given to us when we were ready. She wanted me to discern what resonated with my soul. Now I know what she meant."

"You're very special friends. Emma and I owe you much. Not that I'm with you now because of that, mind you. We're very connected to you and I know we'll always be in touch, no matter where any of us are. Emma sends her love and so do I. God bless you both."

Mary's image faded away and Ellen and Chris slowly became aware of their surroundings, definitely more enlightened and somewhat overwhelmed.

Safely back in Boulder, Mike and Jesse began discovering new changes in their world. Megan felt she and Steve were not quite in touch with reality. Absolutely nothing was the same. Everything looked, sounded, and even smelled different.

Steve was intent on organizing and protecting his tribe. Catching each other's thoughts created some strange conversations, but most of Jesse's thoughts remained enshrouded in fog. One minute he was leaping around the beautiful lush yard with the other kids, and the next he appeared to be lost in some deep inner world of his own.

Michael became his brother's protector, much to Jesse's surprise. A new respect had been earned, a strange but comforting feeling for Jesse. He couldn't take Mike on the nightly adventures with Dorado, but his brother enjoyed the far out escapades Jesse shared with him every day as they huddled in their backyard tree house.

Jesse learned much from Dorado, his mentor and friend in the dream world. He was always there, encouraging, reassuring, and loving in his teaching. Jesse recalled the day he had tested the healing techniques he'd been taught by Dorado. Mike had severely sprained his ankle during a raucous soccer ball game and Jesse taught him how to run energy into it. The ankle had taken a couple of minutes to return to normal but the wait was worth the stunned look on Mike's face.

Dorado told him the time was approaching for "the reunion," the spiritual gathering where assignments would be given to those ready to begin their missions. He assured a skeptical Jesse that book learning was a thing of the past because all knowledge was now available simply for the asking.

"Some people," Dorado said, "will be helping those who remain in the Third Dimension. Others will have specific purposes in the here and now. A special few will be dealing with events that will affect all of mankind, the universe and beyond, into the future."

The reunion was to be arranged soon and Jesse's responsibility was to teach his family how to get there, to prepare them for another foray into the world of trans-location. He wasn't sure his parents were ready, but Mike was. Between them they'd make it happen.

Jon, a virtual dynamo of energy, was like a big brother to his "kids," reassuring and guiding them to their families. Many connections were beautiful. Others were difficult, for the children as well as Jon. They had ascended but some were called back into the Third Dimension to enlighten and guide their parents. Most of the kids knew what was ahead of them and they accepted the roles they had agreed to before arriving in the earth plane. Some would succeed. Others would not.

Where Roger would end up had been of major concern to Jon. He had seen the stumbling blocks Roger's parents had set up, and was aware of the dissension between their beliefs. He wasn't sure they had made it through the Shift. Jon guided his friend through the trans-location, and when Roger appeared to his parents out of nowhere, fully transformed and healed with pink cheeks and full head of curly blond hair, they fell to their knees and thanked God.

Jon, overcome with his own emotions, quietly disappeared, knowing Roger was in good hands.

Now he felt that inner need to connect with his own family at Wind Dancer Ranch. He'd visited Ekor twice since they first met and the dolphin's last words had been, "It's time for the reunion, Jon. It's time to go home, my friend." He was right.

Chapter Thirty-one

Julie gazed at the glorious scene from her deck. The Shift had added incredible brilliance and depth to the vista, especially to Crystal Mountain, the imposing mysterious peak in the distant range. Its radiantly beautiful golden aura had always called to her with a special energy, but its luminescence had intensified since the Photon phenomenon. She closed her eyes and opened them again, wondering if she was imagining the shimmering lights surrounding its pyramidal shape. Could the veil that had kept the mysticism of the mountain from her consciousness be lifting?

She wiggled into a more comfortable position and left her body even before beginning her meditation.

Swept into a vortex of energy, it lifted her through time and space. A gust of wind swirled around her and she heard the word "reunion." Out of the trance and back on firm land that wasn't nearly as firm as she thought it was, she called Dave telepathically.

"I thought I'd find you here," he said, rounding the corner of the deck. "What's up? No, don't tell me. I think we've got some work to do."

No one had a clue how the reunion would play out. Julie and her family were to simply issue the invitations.

"It's time to connect with the rest of our loved ones," she began, "but it's much more than that. Our spiritual family extends in many directions. Those who resonate to our vibration will be here. There will be some who have passed on, as well as beings of a higher Light energy, maybe even entities from other planets. They might not look like us, so be prepared for that. I believe we'll be given special assignments to carry out in the years to come. On some level, I expect we know what they are. But even in this dimensional vibration, there are veils that keep us from seeing very far into the so-called future.

"We can't set a time for the reunion since time as we know it doesn't exist now, but everyone will sense when to come. Let's join hands and tune into our own family first, one by one, then send out a blanket invitation to our spiritual group. I'll do a meditation and prayer first. Everybody ready?"

Shifting into comfortable positions, they began deep breathing. Joey's whisper seemed to come from far away. "We'll all be together when the sun rises."

Colors saturated the sky with the sun's first golden ray over the top of Crystal Mountain. Julie was already at the site of the bonfire, an area she considered sacred and protected by the spirits of the land. Joey joined her, followed by Kathy and Bill. Erica bounced along between them, gripping their fingers, dancing to her own music. Dave settled Jeannie and Angela into a comfortable spot. Even Max and Sandy came along, tails wagging with anticipation.

Joey sat in front of the group, very solemn and very grown up. Julie wondered if anyone else noticed how much he had matured in the last few weeks.

"They're coming," Joey announced with a wide grin. "I feel them coming. Uncle Chris and Aunt Ellen are on their way."

The reunion had begun. Thoughts and words and memories were jumbled but when Julie looked into Chris' eyes, words were not needed.

Steve and his family arrived next. It didn't matter how many ethereal conversations had been exchanged; nothing replaced seeing and touching in person.

Jesse and Joey looked at each other, surprised to find they knew everything there was to know about the other instantly. Their connection was deep and strong, filled with timeless understanding. Angela's spirit joined them in their inner world and nodded in acknowledgment of the relationship.

Jon arrived in a swirl of high energy and laughter and embraced his family one by one.

Anna and Doug materialized next, followed by Rachel with hiking boots and a backpack. Julie's dad, her mother on his arm, appeared. Julie's joy at connecting with her parents again brought tears of joy.

Rose materialized next to her great-granddaughter. Dave's father, much to Dave's delight, was finally able to meet Julie and her family as well as his own grandchildren and Angela.

Mary and Emma's booming "Hallelujah" drew shouts of joy from Ellen and Chris, who grabbed them and introduced them to everyone.

Warm greetings continued with entities that looked quite different, but whose energy was familiar.

Jesse and Joey moved away from the crowd and huddled together to compare new discoveries when a voice interrupted. "Hello again, Jesse. And how are you, Master Joey?"

"Dorado! What're you doing here?" Jesse asked.

"I'll be taking part in the events of the day. If that's all right with you, that is," he said with a flicker of a smile.

"Well, sure," Jesse said. Turning to Joey, he said, "Umm, Joey, can you *see* Dorado?"

Joey's mouth had dropped in surprise when Dorado appeared in front of him. "Yeah," he said, nodding. "Hi, Dorado. It's great to see you again." Memories of their time together in past lives tumbled through his head, the amazing journeys through space and lives on other planets.

Jesse put a restraining hand on Joey's arm. "Dorado, can everyone see you now?"

"Not yet, my boy. But they will. Soon enough, they will."

"Then, Joey, you better not hug Dorado. It'll look really funny," he grinned.

Dorado sat down next to them. "As you now know, Joey, I've been working with young Master Jesse as I've done with you in the past and will do again. You've both become aware that Angela's spirit is anything but a baby. Your futures are very tied together."

Dorado withdrew his energy and evaporated. The boys looked at each other in puzzlement.

Julie was the first to hear the wind song in the tall pines. Turning toward the forest and the deepening reverberations, she waited for the advancing gust, for the familiar vibration of the Spirit of the land, the reason they called their ranch Wind Dancer.

"Welcome," she said to the magnificent energy that she knew had something to do with Crystal Mountain. The wind blew on through, leaving a gentle breeze with a whisper of music as a reminder of its presence, a precursor of coming events as the large spiritual family gathered closely together.

Mike, the young warrior, joined his brother, ready to protect him from whatever. Everyone sat quietly, watching and listening as wild flowers danced, birds sang, and the brook cascaded over rocks.

Chapter Thirty-two

Lowering his vibrations to the physical heaviness of the Fifth Dimension, Dorado materialized before the gathering. His physical presence was taller and thinner than humans. His body was hairless and gave him an almost extraterrestrial look. A foggy blue aura surrounded him.

"Do not be frightened," he said. "I come before you in love and peace, to help open your hearts to the wonders of your beginning enlightenment. I am a Gatekeeper, a Master Guide, and have worked with all of you in one lifetime or another, on this or other planets in your universe. You may not recognize me because I appear in various forms, sometimes as a favorite pet or a bird or butterfly. Perhaps I worked with you on a telepathic level, guiding and teaching, depending on the needs of your souls. I have become very close to Joey in many incarnations, and he knows me well. Most recently my focus has been on Jesse, who has been undergoing extensive training through nighttime excursions. He's traveled to spaceships and had metaphysical experiences quite beyond your current imaginations."

Megan and Steve were stunned as puzzle pieces fell into place.

"I am here now," Dorado continued, "to prepare you for the Energy that will manifest before you in a few moments. It is a familiar Energy to all of you, but not to the degree of intensity you're about to experience. You all chose this period in time to return to earth in order to experience, or re-experience, the Ascension. Now it is time for you all to understand, acknowledge, and commit yourselves to your missions, to move forward. Although there is no 'time' in the Fifth Dimension as you once knew it, there is a limited amount of earth time in the Third to accomplish the assignments you will be given. There are many other spiritual families being guided as you are, all with a divine purpose to help and grow, to uncover and discover, to facilitate and teach."

Dorado smiled as he caught random thoughts. "Yes, this *is* serious business. It is also a time of incredible joy and love. Angels will be guiding you as they have been and will be for all eternity. Powers you're not aware of will manifest in direct correlation to your ability to accept and know. Growth of your trust and love must continue to expand, for there are many more dimensions through which you will eventually ascend."

Dorado cocked his head and frowned as though listening, then burst out laughing. "Okay, okay," he said. "I'm being told in a somewhat ungodly manner to zip my lip, that I'm rambling and to get on with it. I can take a hint. Please, my dear friends, get comfortable, center yourselves, and begin your deep breathing. You're about to embark on a magnificent journey. I'll guide you on a meditation that will raise your vibrations even higher so that you'll be prepared for the glorious manifestation of the Archangel Gabriel, who is at this time lowering his vibration to join you.

The meditation was unlike any other Julie had ever experienced. She felt the white light surround all of them.

Whatever transpired would happen to them as a group. A foggy mist slowly enveloped them. Their physical senses numbed as their souls moved, changed, expanded.

Intense blues and purples with patterns of gold filigree swirled in Julie's third eye, forming spiritual geometric symbols. Music more beautiful than she'd ever heard before filled her essence. They were all bound together as one entity, a group soul, individuals but part of the whole. She knew without a doubt that all things were connected, from the tiny ant on a delicate blade of grass to the large black bear roaming Crystal Peak, to Prime Source itself, the God Within. All were One.

Julie sensed a warmth as though wrapped in the arms of a loved one. An incredible brilliance began to grow in and around her and the others. Shimmering, glowing, it began to slowly solidify, condensing to form a presence. Sheer sparkling energy spread vibrations of love that flowed through her being. Feelings of rapture and joy radiated from her as golden beams. And then it began. She felt the depth, the tone, the magnificence of the words.

"I, Gabriel, welcome you in love and grace, dear ones. We, the other archangels and I, are proud of you and know you are ready to continue on your journey of growth and discovery. I have been with you in many forms and ways, and you are recognizing that now. It is a delight for me to join you in this new manner, to communicate and touch your hearts and souls in a way that has not been done before."

Julie recalled all the "conversations" she had experienced with Gabriel through table-tipping and channeling, the guidance she had received and shared with others, opening their hearts and minds to the bigger picture.

Kathy's connection with Gabriel had sustained her throughout her life, talking to him as a friend in the quiet time before sleep. She now knew that she had been with him in the angelic realm for eons, agreeing to descend to the earth plane this lifetime to bring forth her children.

Joey was aware that his unique friend, Mister G, now stood before him in all his glory.

Jean realized that this loving energy was her "doctor" the night of Angela's birth.

"Now, that I have you as a captive audience, it is time to enlighten you as to your missions, your assignments for the time coming. But first we have arranged for what you might call a special viewing window through which you will be allowed to witness the Third Dimension from which you have ascended. The knowledge of what remains behind is important to your understanding of the commitments you are making at this time. You may see people you knew well. Please realize that they have already been blocked from remembering what occurred, and the resulting loss of family and friends. They have been 'adjusted,' you might say, which will make your assignments all the more challenging. This window will feel like your so-called virtual reality. But do not fear. You are safe and will return to this current euphoric state when I summon you.

"Behold, the window has opened."

Chaos was rampant in the city that appeared before Julie's eyes. Fires burned, providing the only light available. There was no power, no running water, no plastic, and no communication. Even now, weeks after the Shift, people remained in a panic, overcome with fear, feeling the world was coming to an end. Small towns, more community-oriented, were in better shape, but fear is fear no matter where it manifests.

Julie heard guns and saw people barricading their homes against marauders. The fear permeating the Third Dimension appeared as an angry red haze wherever there was negativity and denial. The pain she and the others felt vicariously was almost more than they could bear.

Julie's thoughts went to Jerry. He immediately appeared in her vision. Head down, shoulders hunched, he shuffled up one street and down another. Confusion surrounded him and his mind simply couldn't capture what was missing. He jumped behind a tree and crouched as a band of gun-toting gang members ran down the street with loot from a store or house. He slumped against the rough trunk of the oak, heart pounding. Putting his head in his hands, he cried.

Julie's heart ached for her son-in-law. She wondered if it would ever be possible to reunite him with his wife and baby daughter. The answer came to her: *"It shall be given to you according to your beliefs."* Then she heard, *"Beliefs can change if the mind and heart remain open. But it is Jerry's choice. Everyone has choices, no matter what dimension they are in."* And so it is, thought Julie.

Every being at the reunion, in their own way, witnessed the torment and upheaval they had left behind. All felt the dissension, the fear, and experienced a sense of helplessness. The dark side was very, very dark.

Their desire to reach out, to help Jerry and the others, was strong but Gabriel's strength was stronger. The window became foggy then invisible. A feeling of love once again wrapped around Julie and the others.

"You have much compassion for the Third and Fourth Dimensional entities, which is as it must be. It will not go to waste. I will start with you, Julie and David, the nurturers and co-creators of this magnificent family before me. You have taught and guided and loved unconditionally, providing your family with the opportunity to fulfill their purpose on the Earth plane at this time of vast change. Like the tall pines, you have sown your seeds, creating young ones who have grown straight and tall. You will continue as spiritual teachers for the new children.

"Megan and Steven, you have raised two beautiful children, offering them the opportunity to explore, test their strengths and work through their relationships within and without. Unknowingly, you have provided the foundation that allowed Jesse to expand into the realm of his destiny, acknowledging his knowing, his wisdom.

"Michael, a young warrior, has taken on his challenging role and will continue as protector of Jesse and his cousins in the coming years. Continue your support and understanding. Trust that they will be guided on their journey. Listen to your intuition, for it is strong and sound.

"Kathleen and William, or Kathy and Bill as you prefer being called, you have done yourselves proud. You have overcome your struggles, Kathleen, adapting to life on Earth, not an altogether pleasant experience considering the eons of angelic freedom you have enjoyed. And William, your willingness to find your inner child has enabled you to once again become the adventurer you once were. This is an ability you will need to rely on when supporting your own children and the challenges they will face.

"Because of your capacity for sensitivity and complete devotion, you have been gifted with two remarkable souls to raise and nurture.

Erica will find her path, one of support for others, especially women. She has a strong will, a trait that has been kept in abeyance as the enormous power and strength of your son, Joseph, has emerged. I will speak of him later.

"Jean, your goddess energy has facilitated the bringing forth of a beautiful soul, a being who even at birth taught all of you a valuable lesson of trust and healing. Angela's female energy is strong and because of her future path, she will need the abundance of your love and encouragement. Since your husband, Jeremy … Jerry … was not ready to ascend into the Fifth Dimension, you will be given support and guidance from your spiritual family, including your beloved Nana. Your daughter will grow very quickly, physically as well as spiritually, and in wisdom.

"Christopher and Ellen, you will help in nurturing young Angela in the absence of her father. But you have other missions. Your strength in dealing with the Third-Dimensional world has been proven and you will continue working with that realm. Unlike those trapped there, you can travel back and forth, for there is much to do, as you now know. You will find and help those who request guidance, who truly wish to be released from fear and violence and embrace love and forgiveness.

"Jon, you have the ability to spread enormous joy just by being who you are. The support you and your mother share with each other has been a blessing for you both. You're a true teacher, applying your skills through humor, writing, speaking, as well as loving and controlled compassion. Your ability to encourage and assist children who are in pain and dis-ease is a gift given to you to continue to use in this Fifth Dimension and in all dimensions. You will continue to work with children, teaching those who have ascended with their

families. But even more important, you will assist those who have chosen to return to their loved ones remaining in the Third Dimension. They are facing challenges and need the spiritual support you can give them to enlighten their families. Take them on dream journeys; make them laugh. Let Ekor give them rides into the lands of the sea. Yes, it will be possible. Of course, we would expect you to do the same for your nieces and nephews. This will be a much-needed break from the intense growth and learning they will be experiencing."

Gabriel connected with each member of the spiritual family, creating an incredible aura of golden light around them as he spoke. Time stood still.

Gabriel completed his task and paused, as though pulling more energy into himself. Julie was aware of the sparkling vibrations of her grandchildren as they moved toward Gabriel, drawn by an unspoken command.

"Joseph, Jesse, Michael and Angela, you are master souls of a very high level. You have special powers that are now manifesting quickly. You are assigned to a mission that can make a difference in your world, in all dimensions—indeed, in the universe. You will, as all children will, grow and mature very quickly, and your parents and extended family will be there to help teach and nurture you through this period. Your assignment is to uncover the mysteries of the secret pyramids, to release the energies within. This cannot happen until you are prepared. Then you must be ready for unknown forces that were put in place by ancient beings, some dark and some light. Takoma means 'spiritual pathways for beings of light.' You see, my children, the largest sacred pyramid of all is here, well-camouflaged, and it will be known by its golden aura."

Gabriel smiled warmly at his young students and released them back to their parents. Spreading his arms, his blazing aura became even more brilliant, the intense colors expanding in all directions.

"God speed to all of you. We of the Highest Dimension are available to you. Ask and you shall receive. Now and forever, know that it shall be given to you according to your beliefs. It is the promise of God. Go in love. Peace, be still."

Gabriel folded his arms and released their souls. His aura gradually faded as his energy tuned in to higher vibrations. As though in a dream, the spiritual family slowly returned to their physical bodies, descending to what they now perceived to be reality. At last they understood the reason they had been drawn to this glorious part of Colorado, the meaning of their coming together, their mission in the Fifth Dimension. The challenges would be many but they were not alone.

Crystal Mountain glowed on the horizon, casting its sparkling aura up into the sky. The wind whistled through the forest, singing its wind song, encircling Julie and her family with love as they headed for home.

Julie felt a tug on her hand. Jesse, his beautiful clear eyes glowing with the wisdom of the ages, urged his grandmother toward a rocky knoll beside the meadow. From the crest was a clear and magnificent view of her mountain. Hand in hand, they absorbed its intense energy. Sensing the vibrational waves radiating from within, they watched, awestruck, as Crystal Mountain shed its mantle of earth and rock to expose a shimmering golden pyramid. A second structure began to emerge inside the first and then a third, smaller still. All vibrating at different frequencies, they created a living, ethereal painting manifested by a Master artist.

Julie and her grandson looked at each other, silently acknowledging the gift they'd been given. Then the vision faded, the mountain's golden aura protecting the secrets within.

It was the dawn of a new beginning.

"And he said unto me, These sayings are faithful and true: and the Lord God of the holy spirits sent his angel to show unto his servants the things which must shortly be done."

Revelation 22:6

About the Author

Judith Horky has had a passion for the written word since grade school. Raising a family took precedence over pursuing a career for many years, but in mid-life she returned to the University of Nevada-Reno to pursue a degree in Journalism. Her last class was in TV production, and between that and becoming single, her life turned around resulting in a teaching position in television production at the university. This led to freelance work as a producer, assistant director and stage manager.

During this time, a friend introduced her to the metaphysical world. It proved to be another life altering experience sending her on a search for understanding, a spiritual journey that continues to this day.

In 1987, Judy, as she prefers to be called, and her husband, Jim, formed a video production company, Sweetwater Video Production Services, in Los Angeles. After many years of entrepreneurial challenges, they sold Sweetwater giving her the time to fulfill a life long dream. *EarthShift* was born.

Judy and Jim and assorted furry friends now live in Southern Colorado surrounded by sparkling lakes, majestic pines, colorful aspens, and the magnificent mountains they love.